Super Sleuths Book 1: 'The Pirate's Plunder'

by

E. M. Clarke

Pirates! Magic! Spy parrots!
Follow the exciting adventures of the Super Sleuths! Join the twins Zelie and Zav, their cousins Sam and Sofie and their friend Milo as they use magic to solve mysteries. What are the evil Count Zuto and Prince Igor up to? How is the notorious pirate band the Black Cross Gang involved? Can the sleuths save the day? Meet talking parrots and ancient dragons in the faraway tropical land of Sandopolis, where those pesky pirates keep the children on their toes...

Super Sleuth Adventures:

Book 1 Super Sleuths and the Pirate's Plunder

Coming soon:
Book 2 Super Sleuths and the Royal Captive
Book 3 Super Sleuths and the Smuggler's Gold
Book 4 Super Sleuths and the Missing Inventor
Book 5 Super Sleuths and the Magical Parrots of Flambeau
Book 6 Super Sleuths and the Cabin Boy's Secret

Contents:

Captives!

Chapter 11:

Escape

Map of Sandlandia

Chapter 1:

Pirates!

Perched high in a palm tree on the edge of a southern sea, something moved. A glittering of green shone through the camouflage of the palm leaves. It was a parrot. But not just any parrot... Ana was a magical parrot of Flambeau. And she was listening.

The lazy tropical heat lay over everything like a thick blanket, seeping through the cracks of the 'The Slimy Tombstone', the ramshackle tavern which Ana was spying on. She could hear a low murmuring of rough voices from inside. Suddenly, a roar rent the air:

'Might is right, we care for none,
Pay us if you want us gone.
Rise up, pirates! Hear the call!
Plunder, plunder, plunder all!
Ha Ha!'

Ana jumped, feathers flashing. She swooped down to the window sill and carefully peeped over the edge. A terrifying sight met her eyes. Men in dirty clothes, wild beards, and scarred faces slammed down heavy metal tankards, bawling, 'Rise up, pirates!'

Then, all at once, they stopped. A tall figure in a long cloak had risen holding its arms out for silence. Bat-like, the folds of material extended, so the figure seemed to grow larger and more intimidating.

'Us pirates are agreed then.' The voice came from under the cloak, low and menacing. 'We have a deal!'

'So, what's our next step, Vinicius?' asked one of the motley crew, who clutched a nasty looking club.

'Well, Humberto,' the bat-like figure paused, thoughtful. 'I think it's time for me to visit a certain Mr Sergio Huit. I'm sure he'll be very... cooperative.'

At this, the pirates erupted again, whooping and yelling their delight, but Ana was gone. She had heard enough. Up, up into the cloudless sky she flew, an emerald bolt shooting across the city of Sandopolis. A spy heading back to report to her mistress.

***

Zelie Sinclair was lying a short distance away on a sun-baked roof terrace with her twin brother Zav and their best friend Milo.

'Ana's back!' cried Zav. Zelie sat up quickly, green eyes flashing and auburn curls falling untidily around a face shining with excitement.

'Ana!' she cried, as the bird swooped down to land. 'What's your news?'

'Mistress!' gasped Ana as she landed on Zelie's shoulder. 'Pirates!'

'Pirates!' repeated Milo breathlessly, his eyes widening.

'Yes, pirates!' chirped the parrot. 'In league with the Huits!'

'I knew it!' cried Zav. 'I've never trusted those sneaky neighbours of ours!'

'Pa says that recently, the pirates have been even more active than usual,' Milo added. Milo's father was a sea captain, so he knew all the latest pirate updates. The children looked at each other.

'Well, if Captain Jett and Ana think the pirates are plotting something, then I believe it,' said Zelie. 'I hereby call a meeting of the Super Sleuths!'

The children sat together in a circle.

'Elementary!' announced Zelie.

'My dear Watson!' chorused Milo and Zav.

'Correct. If Sherlock Holmes could solve mysteries way back then, I know we can!'

'Well, I'm only ten so I might not be quite so useful,' said Milo cautiously.

'Rubbish!' cried Zav. 'You're only a year younger than us and you've got the sharpest ears of anyone in Sandopolis!'

Milo turned rather pink at this! Zelie continued, 'And we've got Ana who's our secret weapon. Sherlock Holmes didn't have a talking spy parrot, did he?' she demanded.

Ana then chirped up in true spy parrot fashion, 'Vinicius pirate leader! Coming to see Sergio Huit!'

'Vinicius!' replied Milo, shocked. 'Pa's told me about him. He's not just any pirate. He's really dangerous. He's the leader of the Black Cross Gang!'

'And if he's coming to see Sergio Huit next door...' began Zav.

'We're in a perfect spying position!' finished Zelie. 'Places, everyone!'

The children's roof terrace overlooked the courtyard and was encircled by balustrades to prevent anyone from falling off. The gaps between these posts were curtained by pink flowers which grew everywhere. The children peeked down at the courtyard below and waited. Suddenly, Milo's face grew clouded, and he stiffened. 'Listen!' he said.

'What?' hissed the twins, straining to pick up the sound only Milo could hear.

'I – I'm not sure,' replied Milo, his eyes squeezed shut in concentration. 'But it sounds like a long cloak. Swishing.'

'Vinicius!' chirruped Ana, and she flew up to perch on the bamboo shelter to have a better look. The children looked at each other. There were rumours floating around Sandopolis about this particular pirate. Nasty rumours and always the whisper of a long cloak, like a vampire bat.

'He's about to come into the courtyard!' Milo whispered.

'Vile Vinicius,' breathed Zelie with relish as she liked to give baddies nicknames. 'I wonder why he always wears that horrid cloak? He must be boiling!

'Shhh!' hushed Zav, 'Keep watching. And don't move!'

As the children peeked through the veil of flowers dusk was approaching and with it a shadowy figure slunk through the courtyard's entrance. His silhouette cast a dark presence as he advanced, panther-like, through the dusk. Every step oozed confidence, and always the *swish swish* of fabric. As it moved, the cloaked shape radiated an aura of malevolence, an evil which you could smell, touch, taste, and which made the children shrink back in fear. Then, they froze. Vile Vinicius had stopped dead in the middle of the courtyard. He seemed to feel rather than see that he was not alone, and he paused, nose lifted slightly, almost as if he could sniff the children out. Zelie, Zav and Milo held their breath as a ghostly silence fell.

And then, the spell was broken. Vinicius moved on, until he was out of sight, the sinister *swish swish* of his cloak echoing. The children's eyes were wide. They had stumbled on a bit more sleuthing than they had bargained for! Zav gestured to the others to follow him, and they crept slowly down the ancient metal staircase that lead from the roof, testing each step before laying careful feet on them to avoid any give-away creaks. Zav led them down a level to a balcony which was much closer to the street below, and to the doorways of the houses. The front porch of the Huits' house was now below them, and although they could neither see nor be seen, they could hear perfectly.

The low growl of a man's voice reached their ears. "Huit. We meet again."

'Vinicius,' answered a wary voice, mistrust evident in every syllable he uttered.

'It's all agreed on my side,' the rough voice of the pirate rasped through the air. 'Now it's your turn to keep your side of the deal. Is everything in hand for stealing the shipment?'

'Yes,' came the abrupt reply. 'Although morally this is shaky ground, even for pirates.' The voice lowered to a whisper, so the sleuths strained to hear. 'Look, everyone knows Professor Sinclair is motivated by the good of mankind. There'll be a real stink when the key element of his new invention is stolen.'

'Irrelevant!' Vinicius' snarl cut through Huit's concerns. 'I answer to a much higher authority than Professor Sinclair. Prince Igor wants that shipment. Who are you to question the ruler of French Town, the stronghold of the North? You're one of us now,' Vinicius hissed, 'and there's no escaping the Black Cross Gang.'

And with that threat hanging heavy in the warm evening air, he turned, the *swish swish* of his cloak cutting through the night.

The children lay on the balcony above paralysed with shock. Professor Sinclair was the twins' father! He was an inventor, and it sounded horribly like there was a plot afoot to steal an important part of his latest, top secret invention! Before they could move, Ana fluttered over and perched on Zelie's shoulder. 'Stay still!' she whispered, and Zelie put a hand on Milo and Zav, shaking her head.

It was a good job Ana had warned them because Vinicius had not gone. He was standing silently, watching, listening, camouflaged in the growing darkness of the courtyard, waiting to see if his conversation with Sergio Huit had been overhead. Ana swooped around him, trilling loudly and generally irritating the pirate so much that he shot a vicious punch at her. Ana neatly avoided him and retorted with a haughty, 'Pieces of eight!'. Vile Vinicius stared at the bird. 'Pretty Polly!' Ana continued blithely, preening her feathers as if she really was just a normal parrot out for a wing-stretch before bed.

Vinicius' eyes narrowed. 'I don't trust parrots,' he hissed. 'Especially parrots who can talk. I'll remember you,' he added, a nasty grin slashing his pock-marked face. 'Oh yes, Pretty Polly, I'll remember you.' And with a last, sneering glance at the dancing bird, he strode away with a *swish swish* of his cloak.

Chapter 2:

A Little Bit of Magic

As the sound of Vile Vinicius's swishing cloak disappeared, Zav propped himself up on his elbows to sneak a peek at the street below.

'Phew!' said Zelie. 'That was close – I was sure he'd heard us!'

'A bit too close,' confirmed Milo grimly.

'I can't believe Vile Vinicius is plotting to steal Pa's invention!' burst out Zav. 'He really IS vile!'

'And he's working with someone in French Town in the North!' added Zelie.

'The grownups never talk about the North even though they all lived there,' mused Milo. 'Why is it such a big secret?'

'Who knows?' replied Zelie, 'But at least we definitely know that there's a connection between Prince Igor and the Black Cross Gang.'

'And Sergio Huit is in league with them, too!' commented Zav. 'I never liked him but I can't believe our very own neighbour would betray Pa!'

Zelie frowned. 'What a sneak! Who knows what secrets he's been selling to the pirates?'

'And Vinicius is the second mysterious visitor the Huits have had this week!' added Milo. 'Remember the really tall man a few days ago?'

'You're right!' cried Zelie. 'Something is definitely up.'

'Zelie, Zav, Milo, supper time!' an irascible voice interrupted their discussion from below.

'Not a word about this to the grownups,' warned Zav. 'Not until we've got more information.'

'Agreed,' said the other two.

'Ana, go on patrol!' Zelie added, and the parrot nodded.

'Parrot patrol!' she chirped, and she zoomed off to keep an ear out for clues.

'Come on' said Zav. 'I'm a super sleuth who's super hungry!' and they raced downstairs at top speed.

As the sleuths trooped into the kitchen, a delicious aroma wafted through the air, making their mouths water and their tummies rumble. The twins' mother Flavia was just putting the last plates on the table while their cook, Widow Hanlon, dished up.

'What've you lot been up to?' demanded the twins' elder brother Albie, suspiciously.

'Us?' asked Zav.

'*Up* to something?' added Zelie.

'Innocent until proven guilty!' chirped Ana.

'Huh! Picture of guilt!' their brother sniffed, picking up a huge platter of rice.

'Watch this,' muttered Zelie. 'Fairy fee, fairy fee, grant rice invisibility!' And suddenly, the plate and the rice disappeared, just as Albie was helping himself to a generous serving.

'Ma!' exploded Albie, 'she's doing it AGAIN!' and he waved the empty spoon in outrage amid the giggles of the others.

Flavia sighed and calmly waved her hand. The food reappeared, and Albie hurriedly spooned himself a serving, one eye trained on Zelie should she try anything funny again.

'Zelie my daughter,' said her mother, firmly. 'Magic is not to be played with, especially the deep magic of Flambeau. It is a gift; I expect you to treat it as such.'

Zelie looked serious. 'Sorry Ma, sorry Albie,' she said. 'I shouldn't show off like that.'

'No, you shouldn't,' Albie retorted. 'And I still don't see why Zelie's the only one of us to have powers,' he grumbled.

Before Flavia could answer, a tall, well-built man marched in. 'Captain Jett!' cried the twins.

'Pa!' yelled Milo. 'When did you get back?'

'On today's tide,' grinned the Captain as he gave Milo a bear hug and ruffled the twins' hair.

Milo's father, Captain Jett Wheeler, spent most of his life at sea commanding his ship, the Golden Ram. He brought back books found on his adventures to help Professor Sinclair with his experiments. All the technology from the Old World had been destroyed and the knowledge lost. Professor Sinclair was starting again from scratch, using ancient books (which were very precious) and harnessing the energy from the sun.

Hurrying behind Captain Jett was a slightly harassed looking man in a lab coat. It was Professor Raoul Sinclair, the twins' father and the New World's renowned scientist. 'Exciting news mes amis!' the professor cried, taking a seat and eagerly attacking his plate of food. 'We're all invited to an event at the royal palace tomorrow! So best clothes and cloaks.'

The children grinned at each other – a trip to the palace was a real privilege.

'This is a very special occasion,' the professor continued. 'I will be showing my latest invention to the King and Queen!'

'What is it?' chorused the twins.

'It's top secret of course!' Albie frowned. The twins rolled their eyes. Older brothers were *so* annoying!

'Yes, I'm afraid you'll have to wait and see,' their father agreed. 'You know, the more I experiment, the more impressed I am with the technology they had in the Old Times. Thank you, Jett, for bringing their books to me and helping take Sandopolis into the future'. He raised his glass, 'Salut!'

Everyone clinked glasses of cold mango juice, and slurped it down.

'Have you got any books for us this time, Pa?' asked Milo.

'Yes, I have - it's a book about pirates called 'Treasure Island'.'

The three children gaped in astonishment. What a coincidence! A book about pirates – when they'd just heard a real-life pirate plotting with their neighbour!

'Pirates,' said Professor Sinclair, shaking his head mournfully. 'If only they were just in books! They are a real danger to our progress here in Sandopolis.'

'They certainly are,' agreed Captain Jett. 'Especially in the wilds of the North. There's just no order up there.'

Here the sleuths exchanged another excited glance. The North! They must be onto something.

'Have there always been so many pirates around, Pa?' Milo asked.

'Well, not so much in the Old Times but nowadays, because the only way to travel long distances is by boat, we're under constant threat from pirates. And the number of attacks is increasing daily.'

He shook his head. 'Anyway, here's the book,' and he handed it to Milo.

'Thank you for that *delicious* grub, Widow Hanlon,' said Zav, catching their cook around the waist and giving her a hug. Widow Hanlon blushed to the roots of her grizzled grey hair. 'Ah, go on with you!' she scolded, pretending to swipe at Zav with the wooden spoon which seemed permanently attached to her.

The children sat together in their bedroom, Zelie turning the old, yellowed pages of 'Treasure Island' with care. They soon became immersed in a world where pirates ruled and treasure was there for the taking.

'I don't much like this pirate Long John Silver,' said Zelie, 'he reminds me of Vile Vinicius!'

'Except that Vile Vinicius doesn't have a wooden leg,' Milo pointed out.

'How do you know?' retorted Zelie, 'he could have anything under that cloak!'

The children burst into laughter, Zav even let out a couple of snorts, which made them giggle even more. At that moment, Ana fluttered in, landing on Zelie's shoulder. Her bright eyes gleamed as she leant her head towards the children.

'Captain Jett!' she chirped quietly, 'Talking of the North! Danger. Dark forces gathering. Old Times returning!'

'If the grown-ups think the Old Times are returning, that means trouble,' said Zav, no longer grinning.

'We must find out more,' agreed Zelie.

Zav didn't realise how right he was. Trouble <u>was</u> coming. And it was gathering strength.

A hundred miles away, on an abandoned island in the middle of the Great River, someone waited. Pools of muddy water stagnated, water snakes whipped and hissed, and the slow, sinister shape of a crocodile glided by, skin like rough bark, the flash of a predatory yellow eye the only sign it was alive. An ancient palace sat, half submerged in mud, creepers covering it, blocking out the light. Enthroned in the decaying grandeur was a figure, eyes hooded by heavy lids, jewels flashing on the fleshy, ringed fingers which grasped the once-proud throne's rotting arms. And perched on the shoulder of this massive shape, was a bird, shining white, with a sharp, cruel beak, and eyes which glinted coldly.

'Report,' the bird croaked, rustling its gleaming feathers in anticipation. The command was directed toward a greasy pirate who carried a wicked looking club.

'Deal agreed,' Humberto replied, sweating in the humid air. But it wasn't just the heat making droplets of filth drip down his unkempt beard; it was fear. 'Vinicius has reminded Huit of his – er – responsibilities. The shipment will soon be yours. Oh Great One,' he added feebly.

The figure didn't move. Then it started to shake. Great rolls of fat wobbled, shook, and a low, guttural laugh slowly filled the decaying room with menace, accompanied by the 'Caw! Caw!' of a pack of dazzling white birds who had risen, wings flapping thunderously, amidst the gloom.

Humberto let out a yell and flung out an arm to cover his face as the birds' claws rent the air, and the beating of their wings drowned out the maniacal laughter. He stumbled out of the throne room, back out into the sunshine, sweating and cursing.

The darkness was back.

Chapter 3:

To the Palace

Everyone was up early the next day. 'You make sure you wear a dress, Zelie Sinclair - and long trousers for you, Zav!' called Widow Hanlon as she chopped open fresh coconuts for breakfast. 'I'll not have you looking like ruffians up at the palace. And no parrots!' she cried as a hopeful Ana fluffed up her feathers in anticipation of meeting royalty.

'Not this time I'm afraid, Ana,' Zelie sighed, stroking her parrot's wilting feathers. 'I'll see you when we get back.' And with an affectionate nip, Ana zoomed through the window out into the morning blue.

After everyone had breakfasted, the highlight being some of Widow Hanlon's delicious passion fruit cakes, the groom brought round the horse drawn carriage and they set off for the palace. The busy streets were thronged with people, horses, carriages and donkeys, with errand boys flitting here and there. The city seemed bursting with life and colour, the vibrantly painted buildings standing tall: orange, pink, yellow and green all jostling each other shoulder to shoulder on each side of the cobbled streets.

High up, away from the bustle of the city stood the white stone palace watching over its people with a benevolent gaze. This was where King Lucio and Queen Aurelia lived with their daughter

Princess Richenda. They were of the House of Richmondo and had ruled with wisdom for as long as anyone could remember, aided by their Council of Ministers. Sandlandia was a calm and well organised place despite the risks of pirate attack.

The Royal Palace was known as the 'Palace of the Flowers' because it was surrounded by delightful gardens bursting with blooms. This was where everyone gathered for the ceremony, talking excitedly about the Professor's new invention. From the top of the hill they could see the curves of the bay full of ships laden with cargo.

A short trumpet blast signalled that it was time for everyone to take their seats in the golden pavilion for the presentation. After what felt like a very long and very boring series of speeches it was finally Professor Sinclair's turn to address the guests. The children sat up straighter in their golden chairs and gazed proudly up at the stage.

'Esteemed guests,' Professor Sinclair began, pushing his spectacles up his nose. 'It is my very great pleasure to show you my latest invention. It will transform our lives for the better just like the illuminators and the cool boxes we already have. I have called it a Moving Way and it will let us travel long distances quickly while sitting in a comfortable, shaded compartment. It will not use horses as we presently do, or wind power as we use for our ships. It will use a 'power pack' harnessing energy from the sun. At present we have only the prototype to show you, but soon a whole shipment of these power packs will arrive and will allow us to create the Moving Way connecting all the cities across Sandlandia. But don't take my word for it. Come and experience it for yourselves!'

An excited muttering broke out and the crowd of curious observers were ushered towards some very large metal boxes waiting outside. They walked inside one and quickly sat down on the wooden benches. Soon, the compartment began to move forward.

'Wow this is fast!' remarked Zav.

'I can't believe it's moving all on its own!' cried Milo.

'This is what the people in the Old Times called a railway,' explained Captain Jett, 'and each section is powered by one of those solar power packs. It's amazing, Raoul,' he added, addressing the Professor who was beaming proudly. 'When do you hope to have it working fully?'

'By the end of the summer. This little route just takes us around the palace grounds, but once the shipment of power packs arrives it's full steam ahead.'

'Do you think the power packs is the shipment Vile Vinicius is after?' Zelie whispered to her brother as they gazed out of the window.

'It could be,' he replied. 'It's certainly an important part of Pa's invention. Let's keep listening and looking for clues.'

After the Moving Way had delivered them back to the Golden Pavilion, tables had been laid out on the terrace for a celebratory lunch. As they made their way to their places, the twins and Milo saw a girl waiting there. She had long fair hair in two plaits and green eyes.

'Hello,' the girl said, raising her hand in greeting. 'I'm Princess Richenda. I've come to join you for lunch if you don't mind?'

'Of course not!' replied Zelie. 'We've heard lots about you, Princess. Pleased to meet you,' And the three bowed. They all sat down and tucked in to the delicious feast. Cakes and puddings, fruit mousses and even a chocolate fountain crowded the golden tables. It was all delicious and the children ate as much as they could.

'I'm stuffed,' groaned Zav.

'It'll be ages until the adults are ready to leave,' sighed Zelie. 'They always want to stay and chat. Ooh, who are those people on the top table?' She had spotted a man with long black hair swept back from his brow, a large hooked nose and piercing eyes under bushy eyebrows. He was seated next to two sulky teenage boys who looked like miniature versions of him, and who were shoving food into their mouths in great, greedy handfuls. Their group was completed by a tiny, dark-haired woman with striking green eyes, whose gaze seemed to look right through Zelie, penetrating and mesmerising at the same time. She had seen the little girl staring and Zelie felt the full force of her scrutiny, white hot and searing, as if she was able to see right into Zelie's soul. Zelie stared back, helpless, drawn into the pools of green fire until, with great effort, she dragged her eyes away, rubbing them with her knuckles and trying to ignore the sickening feeling that the woman had somehow invaded her thoughts.

'That's Count Zuto and his wife Countess Rosina from the House of Contuti - and their sons Gergo and Tegel,' Princess Richenda was explaining, not very enthusiastically. 'They're here quite often,' she added, sounding even less happy about that.

'Who are they?' asked Zav.

'They're friends with Prince Igor, a distant relative from the north.'

Milo and Zav exchanged glances. That was the name they had heard Mr Huit and Vile Vinicius mention - the Prince who was plotting in French Town!

'I hope we don't have to meet them,' said Milo. 'There's something cold about them.'

'That's it!' agreed Richenda, 'And it's not just their looks, they're really horrid. I try to avoid them as much as I can.'

'Wait a minute,' said Milo, who was still observing the top table keenly. 'I think Count Zuto has been to see the Huits. Remember, a few days ago before we saw Vinicius there we saw someone else but their face was hidden? Well they might have been trying to disguise themselves but they were really tall, and you can't disguise that. It has to have been Count Zuto, I've never seen anyone that big.'

Zav nodded. Count Zuto was strikingly tall, and he certainly fitted the description of the mysterious caller they had seen at the Huit's a week before.

'Are you alright, Zelie?' Zav added, noticing that his twin had gone very quiet and was slightly pale.

'I think so,' she replied shakily. 'Countess Rosina looks like she sees a lot. She was staring at me, and I felt like she could somehow reach inside me with her eyes...' Zelie trailed off, unsure whether she could explain this sensation, even to her twin. Zav gave her a quick hug and she smiled weakly at him. 'It's a good job Ana isn't here,' she added, 'I've got a horrid feeling that the Countess sees more than is possible.'

'Do you mean – she can sense magic?' asked Zav in a hushed voice.

'I'm not sure,' his sister replied. 'But I do know I wouldn't like to get too close.'

'I've never told anyone this before,' Richenda said slowly, looking wide-eyed at Zelie, 'but I feel exactly the same about the Countess!'

'Really?' asked Zelie.

'Really!' Richenda replied. 'Let's get away from here where we can talk properly. You never know who might be listening. Shall I ask if we can explore the gardens?' The sleuths nodded.

Richenda slipped away to Queen Aurelia and whispered in her mother's ear. She soon returned and smiled. 'Yes, we can go.'

'Do you have a special spot in the gardens?' asked Zelie.

'Yes,' replied Richenda, 'near the moat. You can meet my friend.'

'Great!' Zelie said. 'It's beautiful here,' she added as they walked. 'You're really lucky.'

'Yes, I am,' replied Richenda, 'but it's a bit lonely. That's why I'm so pleased to have met you all. It's this way,' and she led them through a heavy canopy of trees, overgrown with plants criss-crossing each other. As the children moved deeper into the jungle, it cast a green light over everything, giving their surroundings a mysterious, fairy-like feel.

'This is amazing!' Zav cried. 'I feel like an explorer in the jungle, look!' Through the green haze the children could make out a hollow directly ahead, with an ancient red cave carved out of the sandstone cliff which rose up behind it. Swampy pools of water collected in the muddy ground in front.

'Here we are!' Richenda announced. 'Meet Clarence.'

To the amazement of the children a huge creature with a long neck, four legs and a tail appeared from inside the cave. It was emerald green in colour with scaly skin and leathery wings, though in places the scales seemed to be turning brown, like leaves in Autumn. It looked rather like a very large, wrinkly lizard thought Zav, though more fierce. It gazed at them with drooping amber eyes which seemed almost too tired to stay open under heavy, shaggy brows.

'What is it?' asked Milo, shrinking back as it didn't look too friendly.

'It's a he and he's a dragon!' replied Richenda with glee. 'And he can breathe fire. Watch!' On cue, the dragon sighed heavily, took a long, languorous breath and, suddenly, tongues of orange flame jetted out of his nostrils, licking the surface of the pools and casting a red glow over the startled children's faces.

'No wonder there's no flowers growing round here!' said Zav in astonishment. He and Milo had taken a step backwards, feeling very cautious of this magnificent but unpredictable creature. Zelie, however, had moved closer, as if drawn to Clarence until she was standing immediately in front of him, all thought of danger forgotten. The words seemed to come to her out of nowhere, 'Great, good creature; wise and true, tell me what I ask of you.'

The dragon stared languidly at Zelie for a long moment until, to Zav and Milo's astonishment, very slowly, so they could almost hear his bones creaking with the effort, he bowed. And then, hauling himself upright again with what seemed like a tremendous effort and contemplating the little girl who stood bravely in front of him, the dragon spoke.

'Miss Zelie Sinclair,' the ancient dragon intoned in a deep, world weary voice which seemed carved out the very rock which sheltered him. 'Delighted to meet you.'

'How did you know who I am?' Zelie asked, startled.

'Ah, that is one of the great mysteries, child, which dragons alone are initiated into,' Clarence replied, shaking his wrinkled head slowly as if he carried the knowledge of the whole universe with him. 'You are of the House of Sinclair, the female line, and as such you have an extraordinary ability to communicate with animals. You have a special parrot, I imagine?'

'Yes I do, she's called Ana! But how did you know that?'

'All the female line from the House of Sinclair have a magical parrot of Flambeau with whom they can communicate. It has always been thus, and thus it will remain.'

'Well, I know Ana is a parrot of Flambeau,' Zelie replied, 'but where *is* Flambeau?'

'Flambeau is in the far north where, cut off from cities like Sandopolis, magic still rules. These parrots can only talk to their own mistress. No one else. Unless given strict instructions to break that code. Do you understand?'

'Yes, Sir, er, Dragon, Clarence. I know that Ana and her powers are top secret, and we mustn't tell anyone about them, but there's something I've always wondered. Is having a magical parrot of Flambeau connected with my green eyes?'

'Very perceptive, child, yes. I see no harm in shedding a little light for you. Green eyes are rare among humans nowadays, and women who have them have access to more power than they realise. But I'm sure your mother will explain more fully, when the time is right,' Clarence replied stifling a yawn which sent out mini streaks of orange flame from his huge, leathery nostrils.

'Is there anything else can I help you with Miss Zelie of the House of Sinclair?'

'Well, I don't mean to sound too nosey, but why are you here?' asked Zelie.

'To guard the royal family from those who wish them harm.'

'But everyone loves them!'

'Unfortunately, this is not the case,' Clarence sighed heavily. 'There are those who hide in the shadows. The House of Richmondo is never truly safe, so I must remain here, on watch, as their guardian.'

'Is it the Countess Rosina and Prince Igor who are a danger?' Zelie asked.

Clarence paused. 'You are again correct, Miss Sinclair. I begin to think you see more than I would expect from a mere child. I will therefore reveal to you a part of your task: you must help to protect the Princess.'

'Of course!' responded Zelie eagerly. 'We'll do anything we can to help. We're friends already - and she has green eyes like me!'

'Yes,' agreed Clarence slowly, the light flaring in his amber eyes. 'Yes, indeed she does. And Miss Sinclair, the Princess also possesses powers like yours.' Zelie's eyes widened, but before she could speak, Clarence continued in a serious tone. 'But her parents do not know. You must not reveal this – I myself have made Richenda aware of some of her power but the King and Queen must remain ignorant for everyone's safety. Do you understand?' and the dragon asked the last question so fiercely, that Zelie shrank back slightly away from the tongue of flame which leapt from Clarence lips.

'Yes, yes of course,' she replied. 'I promise!'

'Good. I feel you are one to be trusted,' replied the dragon, calm once more.

Zelie smiled, 'I'm so pleased to have met you,' she said, and she gave a little bob of a curtsey.

'It is always a privilege to meet one of the owners of the parrots of Flambeau,' replied the dragon, gravely. And with a brief bow, he turned slowly and lumbered back into the shelter of his cave.

During this encounter, Zav and Milo had been watching Zelie's fearless behaviour full of admiration. She had never seen a dragon before but she had felt a strange kinship with Clarence. It just hadn't occurred to her to be scared. Zav looked at her with pride. His sister wasn't afraid of anything.

'What were you doing?' asked the other children, when Zelie finally came back to the group.

'Just asking my friend Clarence a few questions,' Zelie replied, casually.

'Your friend Clarence!' Zav exclaimed.

'How can you talk to him?' asked Milo.

'I just can,' said Zelie. 'It's funny I don't even realise it, but words just come to me out of nowhere.'

'You have magical powers,' the Princess observed. 'Me too! I have the power to make animals speak to me - Clarence taught me a magic rhyme.'

'Me too!' replied Zelie. The two girls looked at each other with respect.

'I'll definitely ask my parents if I can see you again,' said Richenda, smiling broadly.

'Listen!' hissed Milo, holding up his hand in alarm, his urgent whisper cutting through the companionable atmosphere. The children fell silent, and then they heard the unmistakable sound of heavy, clumsy movements breaking through the lush ferns which carpeted the way to Clarence's cave.

Richenda went pale. 'This is my secret part of the garden – no one is permitted to come here!'

Zav ran back a few metres and took up a defensive position using one of the creeper-wrapped trees as a shield. He peered out from its shelter carefully, then came sprinting back. 'It's those horrid looking boys we saw at the feast, the Count and Countess' sons.'

'Gergo and Tegel!' Richenda gasped, running to the open mouth of the cave, gesturing for the others to follow her. 'Clarence!' the sleuths heard her whisper, her voice laced with fright. As Zelie, Zav and Milo sped into the cave's entrance they saw the ancient creature listing intently to Richenda, his head bowed and his eyes narrowed. He glanced up at the children and ushered them to stand behind his worn wings.

As they crouched there, water dripping from the jagged ceiling of red stone, they heard an increasingly loud crashing, accompanied by dissatisfied, argumentative voices.

'YOU were the one who said let's follow them!'

'I was NOT! YOU saw them leave, YOU made me come here and now I've fallen over these stupid plants and I HATE it!'

'Stupid nature!' the nasal voice agreed.

'I can't even SEE them anyway, they could be ANYWHERE!' rejoined the moaning voice, his dull tone seeming to flatten everything in its path as effectively as his heavy footed tramping.

Clarence sighed heavily, his entire leathery body seemed to be rolling its eyes at the stupidity coming in waves towards him.

'Stay back!' he commanded in a hushed tone. 'And watch this.'

Clarence's yellowed claws scooped up a few dark green leaves from a basket leaning against the wall of the cave and popped them delicately in his jaws. Strange time for a healthy snack, thought Zav. And then, Clarence was breathing smoke through his nose and mouth through the leaves, igniting something in the foliage he was chewing creating an extraordinary thickness to the texture of the smoke which escaped in wreaths from his mouth and nostrils. A fragrant herbal scent filled the air, and as the children gazed past the dragon's aged form, they realised that they could no longer see the greenery, or the swampy puddles, or the pathway leading through the canopy.

'Magic!' breathed Milo, awestruck.

'Where *are* we?' the high, wheedling voice was back. 'I can't see anything. Gergo, where ARE you?'

'*I* don't know, do I?' the flat voice responded, 'I can't see ANYTHING! This is your fault, Tegel! Let's go and spy on the Princess you said. Huh!'

'Oh shut up!' snarled his brother. 'This is a complete waste of time. And I've ruined my new trousers.'

'Who CARES about your new trousers?' mocked Gergo. 'I'm leaving! Find your own way back!'

And with that, there was a tremendous crashing, rather like a clumsy elephant buffeting its way through the thick foliage.

'Wait! Gergoooo!' shrieked Tegel. And, slowly, the quarrelsome voices faded away.

Clarence turned and smiled smugly at the four children, mouths open at the closeness of their escape. 'I may have lost my ability to fly, and various other bodily functions,' the dragon said, 'but there are a few tricks I can play even now. On you go, children, it is safe. Take care.'

'Thank you, Clarence, thank you!' the children said gratefully, as the smoke started to clear and they made their way through the eerie green glow of the canopy again.

'Princess,' muttered Zelie urgently as they walked, 'now you must believe Clarence when he says that the House of Contuti and Prince Igor wish you harm.'

Richenda nodded. It was certainly not news to her, and the attempted spying by Gergo and Tegel had been further proof. 'But there's something else,' the Princess said, tears filling her eyes, 'Prince Igor is coming on a royal visit here soon!'

'Don't worry, we'll find out all we can about Prince Igor, and the Count and the Countess,' promised Zav, who had joined the girls and overheard their conversation. 'We're Super Sleuths after all – we love nothing better than to solve mysteries. We're off to the port tomorrow so we'll try to pick up some clues there.'

'That would be wonderful,' replied Richenda, smiling weakly at him. 'You and Milo did a fantastic job warning us about those idiotic spies!' she sniffed, 'I wish I could join in but I'm never allowed to leave the palace.'

'We could make you an honorary member?' offered Milo.

'Great idea!' chimed in Zelie, 'You're in! All you need is the secret password which is 'Elementary'. And the reply is -'

'My dear Watson!' chorused Milo and Zav.

'Elementary, my dear Watson,' repeated Richenda, her eyes sparkling - this time with happiness rather than tears. And with that, they all shook hands to seal the matter.

Chapter 5:

More Pirates at the Port

Early the next morning, Captain Jett Wheeler
escorted Zav, Zelie and Milo to Sandopolis port for their trip to see
their cousins in Red Cove. The children were bouncing with
excitement as their carriage made its way across the bumpy
cobblestones of the city, not just about their holiday and fun with
the cousins, but also about visiting the port itself and the
opportunity to do some sleuthing. It was all part of the adventure,
as they weren't allowed to go very often due to the pirate menace.
They wound their way down through the bustling
town, the pathways growing narrower and narrower as they moved
towards the dock.

Their horse slowed to walking pace as they rounded a corner onto
the crowded quay. There were hordes of sailors singing sea
shanties raucously as they worked on the huge ships
moored where Captain Jett's vessel, the S. S. Golden Ram, was tied
up with its cargo being loaded. The air sang with a medley of shouts
and frequent bellows of laughter, while the sails of the ships
fluttered in the breeze like white feathers. Through the melee the
children spotted their friend Hector, the Golden Ram's cabin boy,
and waved furiously at him.

'I've got a few jobs to do onshore so go along to 'Three Men in a Boat' on the hill and I'll meet you there,' said the Captain, referring to a busy pub which was a favourite of sailors. 'Have a juice and a cake and tell Finn McClure it's on me. I'll get there as soon as I can.'

The children exchanged delighted grins: they relished an opportunity to watch what was happening in the bustling port, especially if it involved cake! And after all, thought Zav, if they aimed to be super sleuths they needed some more spying practice.

'Let's sit in the window so we can have a good look at everything!' suggested Zelie.

The ancient houses that jostled against each other, all higgledy-piggledy, had lots of nooks and crannies hidden inside them. Many had a bay window that curved out into the street so the sailor's family could have a good view of the ships as they waited to greet a returning family member from their long voyage at sea.
Finn McClure the landlord had bundled cushions into his window seat to provide extra comfort while his guests watched the world go by.

The children trooped into the pub, Ana perched happily on Zelie's shoulder, and were greeted with a cheery, 'Hello me hearties!' from a pink-cheeked man as round as he was tall, his striped apron groaning at its strings as it attempted to stay tied around his magnificent girth. 'A wee sweet treat for yous is it?'

'Yes please, Mr McClure,' replied Zav, giving the landlord a mock salute.

'Coming right up you young scallywags!' Finn answered with his customary good humour, and he waddled back to the bar to rustle up something delicious.

'This is a treat,' remarked Milo as they devoured moist squares of orange cake, washed down with foaming tankards of iced passion fruit juice. 'I could stay here forever! It's a feast for the eyes – and tummy!' There were many ships loading and unloading silks, cotton and a myriad of spices whose rich smells came wafting through the open window.

Milo produced a small eye glass. 'Pa said it was a spare,' he explained. 'We can use it to see better, especially long distances, like they do on the ships.'

'Cool!' said Zav, 'what can you see?'

'Oh no!' Milo almost dropped the eye glass in his shock. He pointed towards the dock, 'is that Vile Vinicius?'

'Where?' hissed Zav, grabbing the spy glass and pointing it in the direction of Milo's outstretched arm.

'Down by the dock!' All three children stared in the direction Milo was pointing and, sure enough, there was the distinctive cloaked figure of Vile Vinicius talking to a disreputable looking sailor dressed in filthy clothes with a vicious looking knife at his belt.

'I'm glad we're up here,' remarked Zav, passing the spy glass to Zelie. 'We can spy on him without being spotted! Have you noticed that people never look up when they're checking no one is watching them? They look to the sides but never upwards.'

'Good point,' said Zelie, 'that's probably why they don't notice Ana.' She whistled softly and the parrot flew over from one of the rafters above the bar where she had been perching, her bright eyes keenly scanning the drinkers in the pub. She landed delicately on Zelie's shoulder and gave her vivid green feathers a little shake.

'Go and listen, Ana,' Zelie said, in a low voice, gesturing towards Vile Vinicius standing on the dock. Ana flew off, an iridescent shimmer in the sunlight, looking as much a part of nature as the other birds around her.

'It's a good job we've got Ana,' remarked Zav.

'I wonder who Vile Vinicius is talking to?' mused Milo looking through the eye glass again.

'He looks seriously fishy!' declared Zav.

'Fishy? Try filthy!' added Zelie, wrinkling her nose up in distaste. 'I'm surprised we can't smell him from here!' The three children giggled.

'Let's call him Filthy Fernando!' Milo suggested with a cheeky gleam in his eye, and the sleuths giggled even more.

'Vile Vinicius, Filthy Fernando – we're building up quite a collection!' remarked Zav.

After a few more minutes, Vinicius and his sinister sailor companion split up and Ana came zooming back up to re-join the children.

'Zav, you follow Vinicius and Milo, you track Fernando,' said Zelie quickly. 'I'll get the information from Ana.'

'Roger that!' the boys responded, and they scrambled off the cushions and headed for the door.

'Could you hear anything?' Zelie whispered to Ana, giving her a stroke.

'Stolen shipment! Goods plundered!' Ana squawked urgently. 'Hidden away!'

'Oh no,' Zelie breathed, 'that means Vile Vinicius' plan is going full steam ahead! But what can we do? I hope the others can find out more!'

And that was just what Zav was trying to do! He had slipped after Vile Vinicius, keeping himself in the shadow of the thick stone walls, flitting behind the pirate like a ghost. The *swish swish* of Vinicius' cloak led him to the ancient oak doors of The Slimy Tombstone, the most notorious pub in town and one forbidden to the children. Even Captain Jet wouldn't set foot in it. Zav faltered as he watched his quarry disappear into the shadowy entrance. As Vinicius pushed open the heavy, creaking door the sound of raucous laughter, shouts and the slamming of tankards on the battered wooden bar filled the street:

'Fifteen men on a dead man's chest,
Yo ho ho and a bottle of rum!'

Zav shivered even in the heat of the day. That was a pirate song. And pirates were very bad news. He jumped as a hand touched his shoulder and spun round, ready to run for it. He sighed with relief as he looked into the green eyes of his twin who put her finger on her lips. Together, they moved quietly back round the corner.

'He went into the Slimy Tombstone,' said Zav.

'Definitely up to no good then!' declared Zelie. 'Even Ana won't go in there. She overheard Vinicius telling Filthy Fernando that they've stolen the goods. It must be linked to what he was plotting with Sergio Huit.'

'This looks bad,' Zav replied, frowning slightly. 'Where's Milo?'

'Still tracking Filthy Fernando,' said Zelie. 'We'd better see if he's found anything out.'

The twins quickly retraced their steps back through the winding streets towards the dock. As the hubbub grew louder, they turned a corner and found themselves facing the bustle of the harbour.

'There!' hissed Zav. 'Filthy Fernando, talking to that other sailor down by the quay.'

'That's the sign of the Black Cross Gang they're wearing!' exclaimed Zelie in horror, seeing the inky black cross tattooed on the men's necks.

'Where's Milo?' whispered Zav, urgently. 'If they're from the Black Cross Gang this is really dangerous!'

Suddenly, Filthy Fernando stopped talking to his companion and lunged towards a pile of wooden crates covered in sacking. A high pitched squeal cut through the air as he pulled Milo out by the collar of his t-shirt! Zelie's mouth opened in a gasp of fear and she clutched her twin's hand, powerless, as Milo was dragged, kicking and shouting, towards the boardwalk of a ship with black sails, the flag proudly proclaiming it as 'The Black Vulture'.

'Teach yer to spy on ME!' roared Filthy Fernando, in a voice quite as hideous as his appearance.

'No!' Milo screamed, 'Get OFF!' and, with a superhuman effort, he wrenched himself from the sailor's filthy grasp, ripping his shirt in the process but managing to wriggle free. The sailor grabbed at him once more, a roar of anger filling the air, but he was too slow. Milo was sprinting away from the dock, towards the narrow streets and the safety they provided, propelled by the vicious threats which rang through the hot summer air. Zelie and Zav rushed after him, finally catching up with him near the Three Men in a Boat.

'Oh, Milo!' Zelie cried, and flung her arms around him.

'That was close!' grinned Zav, slapping his friend on the back. 'Thank goodness you managed to shake him off!'

'Thank goodness!' agreed Milo. 'I don't think I've proven myself to be much of a Super Sleuth today,' he added, ruefully.

'Well, we can't always be super all the time!' Zelie replied, bracingly, and she grinned at him, her green eyes sparkling. 'Bet you're the only person who's ever managed to escape Filthy Fernando!'

Milo smiled. 'I did overhear something useful though,' he said. 'The Black Cross Gang are definitely involved with Vinicius' plan, and it's something to do with their Headquarters near Red Port!'

'And Ana overheard that they've successfully stolen the shipment they were after,' interrupted Zav.

Milo's eyes widened, 'I also heard Filthy Fernando boasting that some of the Council of Ministers are involved.'

'Whoa!' remarked Zav. 'That means this goes all the way up to the top! I wonder if King Lucio knows some of his Ministers are in league with a gang of pirates?'

'He can't do!' exclaimed Zelie.

'And that's a really useful clue about the pirates' headquarters being near Red Port,' Zav continued. 'It's a wild coast up there with mangroves and small islands and all sorts. A perfect hiding place! It'll be tricky to find.'

'We can search when we're in Red Cove with the cousins!' said Zelie excitedly. 'With Sam and Sofie to help we're bound to discover something. This is turning out to be a very eventful first case for the Super Sleuths!'

Milo shook his head, 'If the pirates in the Black Cross Gang catch us it might be the last.'

Chapter 6:

Cousins at Red Cove

Later that day, three children, a parrot and a disgruntled looking Widow Hanlon (who had arrived with all the luggage) boarded The Golden Ram, finally ready to set off for Red Cove. As they marched on deck, they sang cheerily:

'A sailor went to sea, sea, sea
To see what he could see, see, see,
But all that he could see, see, see
Was the bottom of the deep blue sea, sea, sea!'

Widow Hanlon raised her eyes to heaven. 'Being on a boat is bad enough but this'll feel like a very long voyage if yous carry on singing that ditty!' she remarked, drily. At which point, of course, the sleuths launched into an even louder rendition! Muttering crossly about disobedient children and irritating sea shanties, Widow Hanlon made her way below decks.

'All aboard!' Captain Jett yelled.

'Ay aye, Cap'n!' the children responded their voices whipped away by a vigorous wind which had started blowing. Ana had zoomed off to fly above the boat in the slip stream with the gulls and other seabirds.

'Let's go and see the Quartermaster and check on the provisions!" said Zelie.

'Yes, let's!' agreed Zav. 'Captain Jett's sailing straight off from Red Port after he's dropped us off so there will have to be plenty of supplies to keep the men fed and watered.'

The children scurried along the deck, dodging sailors hauling up huge sails, and waving at any of the men they knew. They even spotted Hector the cabin boy, very high up, scaling the rigging and swinging between sections effortlessly, like an acrobat performing to an invisible crowd. The sailors sang as they worked, heaving their cumbersome ropes and equipment to the steady beat:

'There were rats, rats,
as big as bloomin' cats,
in the stores, in the stores, in the stores!
There were rats, rats,
as big as bloomin' cats,
in the quartermaster's stores!"

The children joined in, stamping, clapping and singing just as loudly and raucously as any sailor.

'We'll have a rat as big as a bloomin' cat please Quartermaster!' Zav declared when they reached the stores. However, he had to make do with a traditional ship board meal of biscuits and dried meat, which was so tough you had to suck at it to make it at all chewable.

'How about a spot of that there rum, me hearty?' suggested Milo hopefully.

'Get away with you, now!' scolded Widow Hanlon, affectionately, and the Quartermaster roared with laughter, the tears running down his wind-ravaged cheeks.

Captain Jett soon entered the storeroom, ducking under the low beam and unrolling a big, yellowed map of heavy parchment. 'Here's our route,' he explained, tracing it with a fingernail. 'We'll head out to the bay by the light house at Fairlight and then along the Coconut Coast. We'll go past Lookout Point to Red Port. It dates back for hundreds of years and us sailors have always used it as a safe port for trade.'

'Why does the map stop there?' asked Milo, curiously, pointing to a blank section just above Red Cove.

'For the simple reason that there are no maps of the north,' Captain Jett replied, seriously. 'And there's even more pirate activity around there because of that! Not to mention the offshore islands and mangroves which provide perfect camouflage. It's a wild spot.'

'Perfect place to hide a bit of pirate's plunder!' remarked Zav, his eyes lighting up.

Suddenly there came a sharp cry of 'Land ahoy!' from the crow's nest. They were approaching Red Port! The sleuths dashed up onto deck and leaned over the side of the boat, salty sea spray stinging their faces as they gazed out at the red cliffs which gave way to the Red River which wound its way inland.

'I love the way Red Cove and Red Port are named after the colour of the rock!' shouted Milo over the wind and sea spray. 'Look at those cliffs! There must be so much iron in them to make them that red!'

The ship weighed anchor and the children swung themselves down into the Golden Ram's long boat, Ana once again perched on Zelie's shoulder. Widow Hanlon clambered in after them, and when they were all nestled comfortably the sailors heaved to, their arms straining at the oars. Red Cove was on the opposite side of the river to the port, but with Captain Jett's strong-armed crew at the helm, it was easy to row across. The children jumped out of the boat as soon as it touched the white sand, saluting Captain Jett smartly and shouting their thanks to the sailors, who grinned back at them. Widow Hanlon followed weighed down with supplies rather like one of the donkeys you found everywhere on this part of the coast and looking very relieved to be back on land. She resisted all attempts the children made to help, simply saying, 'Go on with yous! You're here for the beach, and that's where yous should be. Run off with you now!'

So, the children picked up their bags and headed towards the beach house, its high white walls shining. They could hear the wind in the palms and the calling of little green parrots, soothing and peaceful, especially after the bustle of Sandopolis.

'I always forget how pretty it is here!' sighed Zelie, happily.

'And how quiet!' added Zav.

'Sandy roads,' observed Milo. 'Much quieter than the cobblestones in the city.'

The motto 'Familia Omnes' ('family is all') hung proudly on the wall of the house. The sleuths dumped their rucksacks on the brightly tiled floor and raced up to the veranda where colourful hammocks hung ready to be occupied by sandy bodies. The children could see the turquoise water lapping at the shore and the ships dotted on it.

'May holidays last forever!' cried Zelie, and she spun round and round, arms outstretched and chin tilted towards the sun.

'Ahoy there!' came a shout from below, and the sleuths turned quickly to look over the balcony, grins splitting their faces as they saw their cousins, Sofie and Sam. Sam was a year older than the twins and Sofie was a year younger, like Milo. The cousins were very alike with a riot of curly dark hair; they looked a lot like Zav. The family joke was that he and Sam were more alike than he and his twin Zelie.

The children pelted down the steps and out into the courtyard, grabbing their cousins round their waists and swinging them round.

'We've missed you!' Sofie cried, giving Zelie an extra hug as the boys shook hands vigorously.

'And Ma and Pa say we can stay with you all week!' added Sam, grinning.

Zelie giggled, pointing up at Ana who seemed to have found an exact replica of herself and was twittering enthusiastically. 'Ana and Demaria are pleased to see each other, too!' she said. Sofie was also a proud owner of one of the magical parrots of Flambeau, like her cousin, and the two parrots got along famously.

'Wait 'til you hear what we've found out!' Zelie continued, her eyes sparkling with mischief.

'Not here!' interrupted Zav urgently.

'Let's go to the Barnaby tree,' suggested Milo, and they did.

They clambered up their favourite tree, an old gnarled mango with low lying, broad branches just perfect for sitting in and catching up on the latest sleuthing news. The children had been climbing this particular mango tree for many years, and they each had their own favourite branch.

'Now,' said Sofie, her eyes twinkling with excitement, 'tell us everything!'

The sleuths poured out the whole story of Vile Vinicius, his night-time meeting with Mr Huit, the mysterious stolen cargo, the Black Cross Gang and, not least, Filthy Fernando and Milo's close shave.

'Phew! You have been busy!' remarked Sam. 'But what do you think they've stolen?'

'It's still a mystery,' answered Zav. 'We're just hoping it's not Pa's power packs.'

'Well,' his cousin replied, 'if the cargo's hidden around here it'll be to the north as it's really wild. We can take you to explore a new creek we found. Apparently, it used to be popular with the smugglers. If we follow it in our boat, it might help us to find the pirates' hideout.'

'How did you find this creek?' asked Milo.

'Old Pete,' answered Sofie. 'He knows everything!' Old Pete had been a fixture at Red Port as long as they could remember. He had once sailed the Seven Seas in the steps of Marvello the Magnificent and Ignatius the Intrepid who had opened up the first trade routes for Sandlandia. There was nothing Old Pete didn't know about the area around Red Cove.

'And the Lucky Star is ready to sail us there whenever we want!' said Sam, proudly.

'Well, if you're really going to join us in our sleuthing, you'll need to know the password,' said Milo.

'Yes, good point,' said Zelie. 'The key word is 'Elementary', and the reply is – '

'My dear Watson!' chorused Milo and Zav.

'Shhh!' hushed Zelie. 'It's supposed to be a secret password! It's no good if everyone in Red Cove knows it!' The sleuths all fell about with laughter at the thought that, in their excitement, they had given all their secrets away!

'Grubs up!' called a familiar voice, and the children raced back for the feast they knew awaited them. Bright orange crab soup was to start, which Widow Hanlon dished out from a huge cauldron-like black pot. Cheesy buns accompanied it, followed by rice and beans with some fresh fish Sam had caught that very morning.

'Not sure we'll be able to sail in the Lucky Star if we keep eating this much!' groaned Sam.

'We'll capsize her at this rate!' agreed Zav.

'Let's read a bit before bed,' suggested Zelie. 'Captain Jett got me that history book – and there are chapters about the North and French Town. It could be useful for research.'

The sleuths lay about on hammocks scattered all around the veranda. Ana and Demaria flew down to settle on their owners' shoulders, nuzzling Zelie and Sofie's necks. The only sound was the singing of the crickets and the hoot of an occasional owl out to hunt in the gathering dusk as Zelie opened the pages of an old, rather worn volume, its title in peeling gold letters on the front: 'A History of the Keepers of the Parrots of Flambeau,' she read aloud. 'The establishment of the New Era and the years preceding it.'

'Erm, we're the New Era, right?' asked Zav.

'Yes!' replied Sofie. 'When our parents all came to Sandlandia, they established Sandopolis as the new capital, and that was the start of the New Era. So, the 'times preceding it' should include information about -'

'The Old Times!' the children cried. The children looked at each other with mounting excitement as Zelie gently flicked through the yellowed pages. At last she paused and started to read, 'Right. Chapter 7: French Town and the North. The history of the Northern limits of Sandlandia is one of violence, backstabbing and betrayal.'

'Hmm, sounds cheery!' Sam remarked, sarcastically.

'Shh!' hushed Sofie.

Zelie continued, 'No maps exist, leaving the area vulnerable to pirate activity.' The sleuths gave each other meaningful glances remembering the map with all the blank space that Captain Jett had showed them aboard the Golden Ram.

'French Town has long been established as the capital of the North, but it has also been a hub for intrigue and revenge throughout its history. The leader of French Town during the worst troubles in the last 100 years was Prince Percival of the House of Barbosa. Under his rule, chaos reigned and many terrible events took place. The House of Barbosa specifically targeted the owners of the parrots of Flambeau, as they were seen as a challenge to Percival's power.'

Zelie looked up, horrified, at Sofie. Both girls were owners of parrots of Flambeau! It was frightening to think that anyone could wish them harm.

Zelie took a deep breath and continued, 'The House of Barbosa is believed to have united with the House of Contuti and harnessed dark forces in their attempt to gain full control of the area and wipe out any opposition. Percival, who is acknowledged as the worst ruler of any part of Sandlandia in its whole history, had a son, Prince Igor, who is believed to be following in his father's footsteps.'

Not a sound could be heard from the children, who were looking each other, aghast.

'House of Contuti!' murmured Sam.

'Those people you saw at the feast – the ones Princess Richenda is afraid of!' added Sofie.

'Count Zuto and Countess Rosina!' Milo said. 'The Countess who could see right through you, Zelie!'

Zelie was looking very serious now. 'Yes,' she said, slowly. 'And Princess Richenda said they were friends with Prince Igor.'

Another silence fell as the sleuths looked at each other, worriedly.

'And there's something else,' said Zelie, gravely. They all looked at her.

'What?' asked Zav.

Slowly, Zelie held up the history book, and turned it around so they could see inside. The final section of the book had been entirely ripped out.

Chapter 7:

Hector's Discovery

The next morning Widow Hanlon had served up a feast, as usual, and the children wolfed down buttery scrambled eggs, juicy sausages and crispy bacon as if it was their first meal in months! 'Widow Hanon, that was delumptious!' declared Zelie, giving their old cook a big hug.

'Ah, go on with yous,' Widow Hanlon replied, gruffly, but with a twinkle in her eye.

'We're going to row across to the port today,' said Sam.

'Right you are, then!' replied Widow Hanlon. 'But watch yourselves in that wee boat.'

'We will!' everyone chorused, and they traipsed out to find the Lucky Star waiting for them on the beach. They heaved her into the water and set off.

'Now sleuths, the first thing we need to do when we get to Red Port is to gather as much new information as we can,' declared Sam.

'I'll send Ana back to Sandopolis to see if there is anything to report there!' said Zelie. Ana blinked her beady eyes, ruffled her feathers and flew off.

'It'll be very helpful having extra rowers,' said Sam. 'All hands on deck!' And the children rowed for all they were worth.

They soon reached the port, tied the Lucky Star up and jumped out.

'Let's go and find the Golden Ram,' suggested Milo.

'It's over there,' said sharp eyed Sofie.

They marched up the gang plank and were just about to head for Captain Jett's cabin when they heard a 'Psst! 'from what looked like a pile of crates. The sleuths stopped. 'Psst!' There it was again!

Cautiously, Zav crept forward and disappeared round the back of the crates. Then, he popped his head round, grinning from ear to ear.

'Come and see who it is!' he said beckoning the others to join him. The mysterious signaller was their friend Hector the cabin boy!

Hector put his fingers to his lips, and beckoned them inside. There was a sort of space in the middle of the rigging and the crates which he had hollowed out, and it made a perfect hiding place.

'Big news,' Hector said, 'I've been keeping an eye out for anything unusual, like you asked and something is definitely up.'

The sleuths leaned in closer, eager for Hector to continue.

'Yesterday, after we dropped you off, we went to collect some sugar cane from Emerald Isle to trade on our next voyage. On our way back to Red Port to dock for the night, we saw a ship in the distance flying a black cross.'

'The Black Vulture!' gasped Milo.

'Pirates,' breathed Zelie.

'The Black Cross Gang!' added Zav.

'Yes,' confirmed Hector. 'We only saw it briefly, as it was dusk. I immediately trained my spy glass on it to watch, but the strange thing is, the ship just seemed to disappear.'

'Impossible!' remarked Sam. 'Boats can't just disappear!'

'Exactly,' agreed Hector. 'That's why it's suspicious. A ship can't simply disappear so there must be a hiding place.'

'And we sleuths shall be the ones to find it!' crowed Zav.

'Be careful,' warned Hector. 'Those pirates are always up to no good. No decent sailor will have anything to do with them.'

'I also heard that the pirates have formed their own house,' Sofie said, quietly. 'Like the House of Sinclair or Richmondo. But theirs is called The House of Vendetta.'

'Vendetta?' asked Zelie.

'A blood feud,' Sam said. 'It means revenge and a vow never to make peace.'

'So, by calling themselves the House of Vendetta, it's like declaring war on everyone,' said Zav.

'Exactly,' replied Sam.

Suddenly, cries from the sailors went up from outside. 'All aboard!' and Hector jumped. 'I have to go!' he said, 'Good Luck!' and he scrambled away.

'What a discovery!' said Zav as the children hurried down the gangway and back on shore. '

'A disappearing pirate ship,' mused Sam. 'There must be an explanation.'

'Look there's Old Pete!' cried Milo, pointing towards a gnarled old fisherman, his back bent almost double, tending to his fishing nets further down the dock. He was a gentle soul and had the far-seeing eyes and weather-beaten skin of an old sailor.

'Oh, good we can ask him about exploring that creek you mentioned!' said Zelie.

'Ahoy there!' Old Pete had caught sight of the children ambling towards him, and his leathery face had lit up with delight.

'Ahoy! We want to explore the old smugglers' route, Pete,' said Sam. 'The one you told us about.'

'Ah, yes, the creek,' replied Old Pete, rubbing his white-bearded chin thoughtfully. 'Shallow she is, and choked by mangroves round the cliffs. But if you head down it on that there boat of yours, you should be able to moor her and climb the cliff at the end. That'll give you a view all around. But remember,' he added, warningly, 'You must set off at low tide, as I said. 9 o'clock tomorrow morning that'll be – but you'll only have 2 hours, mind!'

'But why will we only have two hours?' asked Zelie. 'What if we want to stay for a picnic or something?'

'Because, young lady, when those tides start coming in the current is very strong – strong enough to pull you out to sea before you can say 'Shiver me timbers',' replied Pete, fixing her with his gaze to make sure she understood. 'Two hours!' he repeated.

'Ok, we'll go at low tide' agreed Sofie.

'No fooling with Mother Ocean,' Old Pete continued as if she hadn't spoken, wagging a bent old finger. 'There's many a poor soul perished down that way in the old times cos they didn't heed the tides. A cruel mistress, the sea. Relentless.' And he gazed out at the blue water, which at that moment was as calm and flat as a lake.

The children glanced each other, stifling their giggles at his rather melodramatic speech.

'Can you remember much about the Old Times, Pete?' Zelie asked.

'I don't like to remember,' replied Old Pete, bluntly. 'They were terrible times. Not to be spoken of. Now you go and enjoy yourselves. And remember the tides!'

'We will!' the children chorused and headed into town.

'Ooh, let's get crab and shrimp!' suggested Zav eagerly. 'I'm hungry!'

'Me too!' agreed Sam. 'Let's go to Molly's.' And so they did.

When they entered Molly's tavern a cheerful voice interrupted them, 'Hello young uns! It must be holidays - what can I get for you?' A round faced, red cheeked lady with streaks of grey in her ebony hair had approached the table, a checked apron stretched over her ample bosom.

'Hi Molly!' the children replied, smiling cheerily at her. They were all very fond of her – they had been coming to Molly's ever since they were babies!

'Well, we'd love the seafood special,' replied Zelie, 'but we'd also love to hear the song, too. Please!' she added, smiling engagingly at the landlady. Molly chuckled and shook her head. 'Go on then!' she said. 'I never can resist re-living the Old Times with a little Irish ditty in tribute to Dublin's fair city. But mind you join in for the chorus!' And with that, she broke into song:

'In Dublin's fair city where the girls are so pretty,
I first set my eyes on sweet Molly Malone,
As she wheeled her wheel barrow,
Through streets broad and narrow,
Singing cockles and mussels, alive, alive-oh.
Alive, alive–oh!
Alive, alive–oh!
Singing cockles and mussels alive, alive–oh!'

The children and the whole pub joined in for the chorus, which had to be repeated several times before anyone was tired of it. Molly smiled, a little sadly the children thought, and wiped a tear from the corner of her eye.

Remembering the Old Times makes everyone so sad,' remarked Milo thoughtfully. 'Widow Hanlon, Old Pete and Molly. Whatever happened to make them flee to Sandlandia must have been terrible.'

'Yeah,' agreed Zav, leaning in, 'but we still know hardly anything about what happened.'

'Or why those pages were ripped out,' added Milo, quietly.

'Well,' said Sam practically, 'We know there was a war and that everyone fled from the old countries to French Town in the North on boats. But then something happened to make our families and lots of other people come here.'

'And that something turned out to be someone!' added Zelie.

'Prince Percival!' Sam and Sofie whispered, glancing over their shoulders to make sure they couldn't be heard.

'Exactly,' confirmed Zelie, grimly.

'I think Princess Richenda and Clarence are right to be worried about Prince Igor if he's Prince Percival's son,' added in Sofie. 'After all, the book said that Prince Igor is following in his father's footsteps.' The sleuths looked seriously at each other.

'I just wish we had more information!' said Zav. 'It's so frustrating having to piece together little clues about the Old Times.'

'Well, there's not much more we can find out about it until someone decides we're old enough to know,' said Sofie, sensibly. 'But we can try and get some different information,' she added, a cunning glint in her eye. '*We* might not be able to safely spy on the pirates, but I know someone else who can.'

Zelie caught her eye and smiled knowingly, but the boys looked puzzled until Sofie gave a whistle and an emerald green bullet zoomed in from the open window.

'Demaria! Of course!' said Sam.

'Let's send her to the Crooked Man and see what she can overhear,' said Zav.

Sofie bent to whisper in her parrot's ear. Demaria cocked her head, blinked, gave Sofie a quick nuzzle with her beak, and promptly flew off the way she had come.

'Will she be ok?' put in Zelie, rather nervously. 'You know, after what the book said about the parrots of Flambeau being targeted?'

'Don't worry,' said Sofie, warmly. 'Demaria has never yet been spotted by a pirate!'

'Yes, she's just a bit cleverer than those rum swigging idiots!' added Sam, making everyone laugh.

Just as they were scraping their plates clean of Molly's delicious crab and shrimp special, Demaria flew back through the pub window.

'Perfect timing!' cried Sofie, stroking her bird's feathers gently to still the beating heart of the parrot, who's little chest was heaving with excitement.

'Pirates! Count Zuto Contuti! Found charts of lagoons to the north,' reported Demaria, almost breathless in her haste to impart the information.

'The Count Zuto we saw at the palace!' said Zav. 'The House of Contuti are definitely involved - ouch!'

Demaria had nipped him on the shoulder. She hadn't finished delivering her news. 'Pirates have password: the ransom is paid!' she squawked, and promptly collapsed onto Sofie's shoulder.

'Fantastic work, Demaria!' said Sofie ruffling her parrot's feathers and holding a saucer of water for her exhausted parrot to sip at.

'Hmmm, it looks like the stolen cargo could be hidden to the north if the pirates have those charts of the lagoons,' said Sam in a grave tone. 'It's the only place they'd be able to hide undetected.'

'Strange that they've been able to find maps when Pa says that whole area is unchartered,' frowned Milo, thoughtfully.

Heads buzzing with this new information and what it might mean, the children back to the Lucky Star. Just then another parrot sped towards them.

'Ana!' cried Zelie.

'Bad news!' Ana cried, flopping onto Zelie's shoulder.

'What?' asked Zelie, aghast.

'Stolen cargo is the power packs!' the little bird replied. 'No Moving Way!'

The children froze. It was just as they had suspected - the stolen cargo *was* the power packs for the new Moving Way. And without them, the new invention simply wouldn't work. More dangerous still, was the fact that new technology had been stolen. Apparently, the ship carrying the cargo had simply disappeared.

'Are you thinking what I'm thinking?' asked Zelie. 'It's just like Hector's description of that pirate ship - the Black Vulture! The cargo has been stolen by the Black Cross Gang and hidden!'

''Poor Pa!' cried Zav

There's only one thing for it,' declared Zelie, grimly. 'To save Sandlandia and Pa's reputation, we must find the den where they've hidden them.'

Chapter 8:

Smuggler's Creek.

The sleuths were up early again the next day, determined to find the pirates' lair. They wolfed down a quick breakfast and boarded the Lucky Star once more. They rowed up towards the spot Old Pete had told them about, timing it carefully so they would reach the opening of the creek in plenty of time for low tide at 9 o'clock. The creek wound its way inland towards the north and the water levels were low enough to allow the Lucky Star to glide smoothly into the narrow passage.

Red cliffs rose on each side of the creek but they were almost invisible, covered with the vibrant foliage of the sea forest. Broad, shiny green leaves reached out and brushed the heads of the children as they passed. Feathery fern fronds tickled their cheeks as the creek got narrower and narrower. The light took on a greenish glow, and everything felt more hushed. The water was crystal clear, and they could see mossy stones and little fish darting between them as they rowed steadily along. Occasionally, the peace was broken by the call of a bird, high on the cliff tops above.

Just when Sam was worrying that the Lucky Star might struggle if the creek got any narrower, it widened into a pool. Mangroves covered the left side, but on the other, a cliff rose up ahead of them, just as Old Pete had described. It looked almost sheer, but when the children looked closer, they could see footholds here and there in its rugged surface.

'No wonder the smugglers used to use this!' remarked Zav, gazing round in astonishment. 'Nobody would know you were here - it's completely hidden!'

'And I wonder what you can see from the top of that cliff,' added Sam, staring hard at it. 'That direction faces North, to the unchartered area.' The children gazed up at the blood-red stone which towered above them.

'Old Pete was right,' said Milo, 'there's no way we could moor the boat on the side of the cliffs, there's nothing to attach her to!'

'Yes, we shall have to tie her up this side, to some of those mangrove roots,' suggested Sofie, practically.

'And then we can wade across to the cliff and climb it. It's pretty shallow,' said Zelie, 'look!' She jumped down into the creek. The water only came up to her knees, and she waded across to the other side with no trouble at all.

'Great!' cried Sam. 'Right you guys, let's get the Lucky Star tied up and head over. Let's push her under the mangroves just in case anyone nosey comes along,' he added.

'Good job we did come at low tide,' remarked Zav. 'It would be tricky to cross this with the water level much higher!'

Once safely across the tidal creek the only way up was to climb. It was hard work; the steep surface made it tricky for them to grasp toe and hand holds, and the sun's rays beat down on them relentlessly, making them think longingly of their cool, shaded journey up the creek.

'Urghhh, look at the ants!' cried Sofie, as a trail of them marched next to her hand. 'They're ginormous!'

'Zelie, send Ana up ahead to be a scout!' called Zav. The little parrot soared over their heads, dipping back down occasionally to give them an encouraging chirrup.

'I wish I could fly,' said Milo longingly as he wiped the sweat from his brow.

'Almost there!' panted Sam, who had nearly reached the top where the stone levelled out again to form a platform overlooking the sea. As each of the sleuths scrambled over the top, they lay panting, gazing at the expanse below them.

'Wow!' breathed Sofie, awe-struck. 'The whole bay is spread out, right in front of us.'

'This is a great vantage point,' replied Sam. 'You're hidden from sight but can see everything.'

'Those old smugglers knew a thing or two,' agreed Zav.

'I can see some sort of roof!' cried Milo, staring hard into the overgrowth behind them, in the opposite direction to Red Port.

'Let's explore!' Zelie suggested.

'We'd better be careful,' Sofie added, warningly, 'the pirates could be there.'

'Yes, we should be as quiet as possible,' agreed Sam. 'Usual formation, sleuths!' The children quickly got into single file, and slipped quietly into the jungle, in the direction of the mysterious roof.

As they moved silently into the coolness of the greenery, an eerie quiet seemed to descend. Even the birds stopped singing as the children edged their way further into the jungle. Soon, the dark, vague shape of a building started to emerge through the dimly lit forest. Sam gave a signal for the others to stop and stay where they were, while he approached with caution. However, he soon waved them over. The building was in ruins, its once proud stone walls had half collapsed. There was little left of the roof that Milo had glimpsed, and a strangler tree had taken over the remaining stone walls so they were nearly invisible.

'I think that tree is the only thing holding the walls up,' said Sofie.

'What is this building?' wondered Milo, 'it's an amazing location.'

'It's very big,' remarked Zelie. 'I reckon it's what they used to call a church. You know, like the pictures we've seen in the old books.'

'Yes,' agreed Sofie. 'The people in the Old Times used to gather in them, didn't they?'

'If it is one of those church things it hasn't been used for years,' commented Zav.

'Look there's a track to the side,' said Sam, pointing. 'Let's see where it goes.'

'We only have a bit of time left,' said Sofie, slightly nervously. 'We won't be able to get back across the creek if we leave it too long.'

'Good point,' said Zelie. 'Let's be quick.'

They walked along the track and on the other side of the headland, invisible from Sandopolis or Red Port, they saw what seemed to be a rocky island.

'I've never seen that island before,' said Sam. 'We must investigate!' But Sofie put her foot down.

'We'll have to come back another time,' she said, firmly. 'Old Pete said we only had two hours, and time is nearly up. We have to get all the way back down that cliff as well.'

'You're right,' said Sam, reluctantly. 'But this is a fantastic discovery! We must come back.'

The children chattered non-stop about the secret island they had discovered, hidden from view, and shared their theories as to smuggler and pirate hideouts. They reached the cliff and made their way down to the creek as quickly as they dared, but as they neared the bottom it was clear that Sofie had been right to be worried. The tide was rising. It was not only much higher, but swirling currents were moving in the greenish water. It looked much more dangerous than the calm, placid pool they had crossed with ease only an hour or so earlier.

Zelie gulped. 'I don't think I can get across,' she said, 'it's too high.'

'Neither can I,' replied Milo and Sofie. The girls and Milo were all shorter than Sam and Zav, so the water was already up to their waists.

'Don't panic,' said Sam calmly, though he did look a bit worried. 'I'll swim across with Zav, we'll get the Lucky Star then pull you up into the boat as we row past.'

'Ok,' agreed Zav. 'But we'll need to move fast – that water is rising quickly.'

'Be ready to jump!' called Sam over his shoulder, as he and Zav half waded, half swam through the increasingly turbulent water over to the mangroves where they had moored the boat. It was quite a battle to get across, and Zav nearly slipped, but the boys managed it, helped by the overhanging roots of the mangrove trees which they grabbed desperately and hung onto, dragging themselves against the current and pulling themselves up into the Lucky Star.

'That current is really strong,' shouted Sam urgently to the other three who were stranded on the opposite bank. 'Climb a bit higher and get ready to jump! We'll be moving quickly. Don't miss the boat!'

'Ready?' called Zav, in position to release the rope tying the Lucky Star to the shore.

'After three!' shouted Sam. 'One, two, three, now!'

Zav released the mooring, and the boat moved quickly away from its mangrove hideaway, propelled by the power of the current and the steadily rising water.

Milo, Zelie and Sofie were ready, and as the boat moved past them, they jumped. Zelie and Milo landed with a thump inside the boat, but Sofie had mistimed her jump and – splash! – she had landed in the creek!

Sam acted with the speed of lightning. He vaulted over Zelie, who was still on the floor, and dashed to the back of the boat. 'Milo, you steer!' he shouted. 'Sofie, grab the oar!' he yelled to his sister, who was trying desperately to swim after the Lucky Star. As he shouted this, Sam flung the oar out to her, calling Zav to help him hold the other end. With a burst of effort, Sofie lunged forward, reaching out desperately and clung onto the end of the oar, the rapids of the now swollen creek pushing her this way and that, as if she were no more than a rag doll. Grimly determined, Sofie hung on while Zav and Sam pulled the oar back towards the boat. As soon as she was near enough, leaving Zav to hold onto the oar just in case, Sam grasped her arm in a sailor's grip and heaved Sofie back into the Lucky Star.

She collapsed on the deck coughing up sea water. 'Told you we needed to get back!' she gasped.

'I'm sorry, Sof,' said Sam giving her a hug.

'That's what I call a close one!' said Zav, 'Are you ok?'

'I'm ok,' said Sofie, recovering as she gratefully sipped the water Milo had passed to her. 'Great team work!' Sofie remarked, her eyes regaining their twinkle. 'It's a relief to know we can deal with an emergency!'

'Yes,' agreed Zelie. 'It's definitely been an exciting morning!'

'A bit too exciting for me,' remarked Sofie, drily. And they all started to laugh.

They reached Red Cove without further mishap, Sam taking extra care to sail the Lucky Star as smoothly as possible. When they arrived back at Breezy Corner, lunch was ready. Steaming platefuls of beans, rice, and fresh fish grilled on an open fire was accompanied by avocado salad. It was delicious, and the sleuths wolfed it down, even Sofie, who seemed to have recovered very well after her adventure. The sleuths decided a calm afternoon was what was needed after the morning's excitement, and decided to search the beach house for anything which might give them any more information or clues.

'I think there might be some old maps somewhere,' Sam remarked. Widow Hanlon looked at them sharply when she overheard what they were talking about, but she didn't seem to object to them studying their parents' old maps, and she pointed out the ancient wooden desk where they were kept.

The sleuths pored over the yellowing pieces of parchment in the cool of the veranda. 'There are still so many blank bits!' exclaimed Zav in frustration.

'They've definitely not mapped the whole area properly,' said Sam. 'There must be a reason. Parts of the map are really detailed – look here at the islands off Sandopolis and all down the Coconut coast. Sand Dollar Island, Crocodile Island, Emerald Isle, they're all mapped on here perfectly. Then, as soon as it moves north, nothing.'

'Pa has lots of the old maps the sailors used in the Old Times,' remarked Milo, staring intently at the map spread out in front of them. 'Some of the symbols are the same.'

'What do they mean?' asked Zelie.

'Well, this symbol means low water levels, and this one is a safe channel. I think this sign means a good vantage point,' said Milo, pointing at the map.

'A good vantage point?' repeated Zelie, 'I reckon that's where the ruined building was!'

'I think you're right!' exclaimed Zav. 'Now, if we take that as the ruined building, we can work out the rest of the map.' There was a silence as four pairs of eyes roved the parchment eagerly.

'But... there's no island marked on here!' said Sam. 'We definitely saw it but it's not plotted on the map!'

'Do you think they didn't put it on the charts deliberately to keep it hidden?' suggested Milo. 'Pa says the old sailors were cunning. Maybe they meant to keep the island off any maps?'

'And this area is a great place to hide anything as the Trade Winds would blow your ship of stolen cargo straight here with hardly any navigational difficulties,' added Sam.

'I've had a thought!' cried Zelie. 'The position of the island would also explain what Hector said about that pirate ship disappearing! It didn't disappear, it hid itself around the peninsula, away from prying eyes!'

'There's only one thing for it,' said Sam. 'Now we know it's there, how about sailing round to the island tomorrow at low tide and seeing if we can get to it by boat?'

'Great idea!' replied Zav, keen as ever for more exploring. 'Look out pirates - the sleuths are coming!'

Chapter 9:

The Hurricane Hole.

Next morning, the sleuths set off to find the mysterious island. It was harder going than they thought and they strained at the oars to keep their little boat on course. There seemed to be a sea fret moving in, a misty moistness in the air descending on the water all around.

'This visibility is terrible,' said Sam shaking his head. 'It's going to be even more difficult to spot our mystery island in these conditions! Milo, keep a sharp look out.'

'Aye-aye, Cap'n!' responded Milo smartly. His sharp eyes were scanning the waves through his eye glass, trying to penetrate the lowering mist, his keen ears ready to pick up the sound of the water moving against the shore of the island they knew must be here somewhere.

'I wonder if it's often foggy here,' mused Zelie.

'It would help to make this place even more secret if it was!' joined in Sofie. 'No maps *and* always misty!'

'And there are ways to *make* it misty, too,' added Zelie, meaningfully. 'You know, magical ways...'

The children looked at each other.

'If this is all connected to French Town and the North, the mist might be to do with the dark forces the history book talked about,' said Sofie. 'I mean, if you can do magic, Zelie, that means other people must be able to as well. And magic can be used for good and evil.'

'Listen!' cried Milo, 'the sound of the water is changing!' The others stopped talking and strained their ears. The water sounded almost as if it was smoothing itself out, like it was no longer crashing against a barrier of land. 'Can you hear?' he whispered. 'That change must mean something is ahead.'

Milo craned his neck forward, eye glass clamped to his face, straining to see what was ahead of them. 'Yes! Land ahoy!' And there, straight ahead, as if indeed by magic, an extraordinary sight was emerging from the fog. As they rowed closer, the details materialised: rich red rock towered ahead of them, hidden until now by the curtain of mist which was slowly drawing apart to reveal the island's secrets.

As they rowed closer, the children stared, awe struck. The island wasn't an island! It was more like an enormous cave with no roof, like a giant had scooped out the middle of the rock leaving a huge opening big enough for a ship to enter easily.

'It's hollow inside!' gasped Sam, rowing even more eagerly towards the phenomenon.

'Pa's told me about these!' cried Milo. 'It's a hurricane hole!'

'A what?' chorused the others.

'A hurricane hole!' Milo repeated. 'They're a really rare rock formations, almost a circle, so no big waves can get in. I had no idea there was one near here.'

'Yes!' agreed Zav. 'You see them near the Great Line which divides the world - ships can ride out storms and hurricanes inside them as they're protected from the waves.'

'And it's a perfect hiding place!' breathed Zelie. They all gazed at the circular island with the rocky entrance ahead of them, its mystery and promise of hidden secrets beckoning them to come closer.

'Be careful rowing in,' muttered Sam, straining the oars against the choppy waves. 'Keep an eye out for rocks.'

Milo turned back to his lookout position, scanning the water carefully as they rowed through the entrance. They left the bright sunshine behind them and entered the cavernous space which stretched before them. Once inside, the waves died down and the sea was very calm. Sunlight spilt down from the hole in the roof, a shaft of light illuminating the natural wonder they had found themselves in. Green lichen grew all over the inside of the hurricane hole, winding itself over the sheltered rock and draping themselves over the sides.

'Wow!' breathed Sofie. Ana and Demaria were swooping round the children's heads gleefully, testing the air currents inside the cave.

'It's certainly a safe anchorage,' said Sam approvingly.

'I can't wait for Pa to see this,' added Milo.

'There's a ship over there!' cried Zelie, pointing. 'At the back, under that cliff of rock jutting out!'

Sure enough, on the far side of the cave there was a ship. A ship with a flag depicting a black cross. The children stared.

'The Black Vulture!' Zav exclaimed.

'Pirates,' added Sam, grimly.

'And if we're right, that's the ship with the stolen cargo,' said Sofie.

'Listen,' whispered Milo, 'what's that?'

They could hear a rhythmic chanting coming from the ship, travelling across the water, the rough, low voices building in ferocity:

'Might is right; we care for none.
Pay us if you want us gone!
Rise up pirates; hear the call.
Plunder, plunder, plunder all!'

A raucous cheer erupted from the ship, accompanied by hoots and yells and repetitions of, 'Rise up, pirates, rise up!'. The children looked at each other, worried and fearful. Hunting pirates had been fun when they were in the relative safety of Red Port, but here in the mysterious light of the hurricane hole they realised that their sailing adventure had quickly turned serious. They were isolated and very vulnerable.

'I don't like this,' said Sofie, nervously. 'Pa has always told us to stay away from pirates, and here we are in their lair!'

Zelie shuddered. 'I'm not getting a good feeling about this place,' she said. 'I think we should go.'

'Plus, we need to get back and tell someone the pirates are here before they spot us!' added Zav.

'I'm going to use the invisibility spell on Ana and Demaria,' said Zelie decisively. 'We know the parrots of Flambeau must be kept secret, they can't risk being seen. Especially not by pirates.'

'Good idea,' agreed Sofie.

Zelie muttered the words, 'Fairy fee, fairy fee, grant parrots invisibility,' and the flashes of green soaring above their heads disappeared.

'Now, let's get out of here,' cried Sam. 'Man the oars!' But it was too late. At almost the same moment the children turned to take up their oars, they heard a hard voice full of menace from the side of the Lucky Star.

"Well, well, well, what do we have here?'

The children froze. They'd been so involved in examining their extraordinary surroundings that they hadn't paid attention to the mouth of the island. To their horror they saw a large rowing boat just off their port bow, flying a similar version of the black flag they had spotted across the water. It must have advanced on them in total silence, using the current to draw nearer to them without the sleuths realising. A short, stocky sailor whose muscles were almost hidden by fat was leering at them, his greasy black hair and beard tangled. He was carrying a threatening looking club, which he was slowly hitting the palm of his hand with, eyeing the children malevolently. His equally unpleasant looking companion bared his few blackened teeth in a horrible grimace as he threw a hook onto the Lucky Star before the children could react, chaining it to the pirates' row boat.

'Cat got your tongue? ' the pirate sneered, rubbing dirty hands together gleefully, as if delighted with his catch. 'Something tells me you're very far from home,' and he grinned unpleasantly at his companion, who wheezed with laughter, his gap-toothed mouth stretched into an evil grin.

'Wait!' said Sam quickly. 'We're allies. The ransom is paid.'

The pirate looked suspicious. 'How do you know our password?' he demanded. There was a silence that stretched into the unnatural quiet of the cave.

'W-we're friends of the Huits!' cried Zav desperately.

'And Vile - er- Vinicius!' added Zelie quickly, her eyes shining with defiance.

The two pirates looked at each other, clearly puzzled by this unexpected information. The first one frowned and turned back to them. 'Well I reckon you're in even deeper trouble than I first thought,' he said with a horrible sneer. 'And what was that flash of green I spied before?' he added, staring intently at Zelie.

'W-what flash?' she asked, bravely staring straight back into the pirate's steel grey eyes. 'There's nothing else here, only us.'

'Must have been a trick of the light,' suggested Milo, helpfully.

'A trick of the light?' mimicked the hairy pirate in a falsely high voice, making Milo flush. 'I don't like children,' he added, menacingly. 'And I really don't like children who tell me LIES!' His voice ended on a roar, making the children jump.

Sofie and Zelie grabbed each other's hands, Zelie communicating with a squeeze of her hand and a minuscule shake of the head that they must not mention Ana and Demaria at any cost. Sofie nodded quickly back at her cousin.

'I've had enough of you, you lying little land-rats,' the pirate continued roughly. 'If you won't tell me the truth, I know someone who can make you talk.' A frightened silence descended over the children. 'You're coming with us.'

Before the sleuths could move, the Lucky Star lurched forwards, dragged relentlessly by the row boat towards the larger ship anchored on the other side of the water. As they drew closer the children could see a small port at the edge of the cave with a rickety looking wooden building built over the water on low wooden stilts. The fat, hairy pirate raised his hand in greeting to a man who had spotted him, raising a bottle of rum in salute.

'Look at his hand,' whispered Sofie in horror, pointing shakily at it. 'There are two fingers missing!'

'Don't worry,' said Zav, quickly. 'Pirates have loads of injuries - they're always fighting!' Sofie didn't look much comforted by this information.

'Let's give them silly names to try and make them less scary,' suggested Milo.

'Good idea,' said Sam. 'Let's call the one with all those black teeth and gaps in his mouth The Dentist!' Even though they were in serious trouble, the sleuths couldn't help smiling at this.

'And what about -' started Milo, but before he could finish his sentence, the hairy pirate was shouting out to the rocky shore ahead of them.

'Look who we found snooping about,' he announced, unmistakable glee in his voice. 'Land-rats!'

'Baby land-rats!' the Dentist added with relish. A figure cloaked in black was standing on the rocky shore, slightly apart from the other men, his face turned away. But at this, he turned slowly and with a jolt of horror, the children saw Vile Vinicius staring coldly at them. The children shivered.

'Spying scurvy knaves!' the hairy pirate spat, shaking his fist at them for good measure.

'Rapscallions! Scoundrels!' continued his toothless pal.

Vinicius held up a hand, and he fell silent. The cloaked figure gazed at the children as the boats knocked gently against the shore, a nasty grin spreading across his face.

'So,' he said with quiet menace. 'Been a little bit too clever for our own good, haven't we?'

Chapter 10:

Captives!

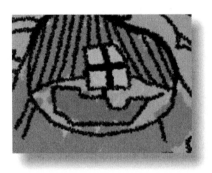

Vile Vinicius was staring at the children. 'Bring them ashore,' he ordered. 'Search them, then throw them into the brig!' The sleuths exchanged worried glances. The brig was what sailors called the prison. Zelie felt a flutter by her shoulder, and was reassured. Ana and Demaria were nearby but still invisible, hidden from the pirates. The Dentist forced the children into a line and marched them onto the rocky shore.

'Turn out your pockets,' Vinicius ordered. He had no need to shout, menace was evident in every quiet syllable he uttered. The children did so. Amongst the string and other bits and bobs were Sam's penknife and a flash of bronze drew attention to Milo's spyglass which he clutched in his hand.

'You,' whispered Vinicius, pointing at Milo. 'You've got something I want, boy.'

Milo stood stock still, terrified. Vinicius took a step towards the smallest sleuth.

'Leave him alone, you big bully!' cried Zelie hotly and she stood in front of Milo, as if to protect him.

Vinicius laughed coldly and gestured towards Humberto, who swiped Zelie aside with a swift blow, as if she were no more than an irritating fly buzzing around. She staggered, but Zav caught her and glared furiously at the men. Humberto grabbed the eye glass from Milo and brandished it so Vinicius could see.

'I've wanted one of these for a long time,' Vinicius said gloatingly. 'So kind of you to share.'

The children stared back at him defiantly, determined not to show him even the slightest glimpse of fear. Then, they heard a strange rattling moving closer and closer. Rattle. Rattle. Rattle. An emaciated, mangy looking cat with one beady red-rimmed eye had appeared. Its moth-eaten coat of black fur had tufts ripped out of it, as if it was always fighting, and it was sidling up to the children, hissing at them. Around its neck hung a necklace of bones. With each step it took, the bones clattered against each other, making the sinister rattle the children had heard.

'Ooh, Rattling Cat wants to see her new visitors!' exclaimed Humberto. But almost before he could finish his sentence, Rattling Cat had jumped up with a snarl and swiped viciously at the air near Zelie's shoulder - the exact spot where Ana had been hovering, invisible, just a few seconds earlier. Zelie gasped and drew back, away from the cat who was hissing and spitting its fury, its one remaining eye swivelling round desperately in its socket, staring madly at the sky.

'What is it, Rattling Cat?' asked Vinicius, his eyes glinting. 'What can you smell? What's there that we can't see?'

'I thought I saw something in the air when I grabbed them,' added Humberto. Vinicius' scanned the air, eyes narrowed, as if trying to see between the molecules above him. Zelie held her breath. 'Stay away Ana and Demaria!' she repeated silently to herself.

Rattling Cat was still hissing and occasionally swiping at nothing, the bones of her necklace clattering against each other menacingly. But nothing happened. Vinicius stopped sweeping his gaze across the sky abruptly. 'Hmmm. Interesting. Anything to say, children?' he asked, taking a step towards Zelie, his face twisted into an ugly snarl. 'I'm sure you have an explanation,' he added with soft menace.

'Not to you!' replied Zelie, defiantly.

'Oh, how courageous,' mocked Vinicius. 'Perhaps a night in the brig will soften you up and make you more willing to talk,' he said, smiling horribly. 'Lock them up!'

'You'll be sorry you messed with us!' added Humberto, as he shoved at Sam, who was at the front of the line, to start walking towards the shack on stilts and up the roughly hewn steps.

'Please don't,' said Sofie desperately, following her brother. 'Please let us go.'

'Ha! Not on your life, Missie,' responded Humberto. 'The Black Cross Gang is the scourge of the seven seas, known for our brutality,' he continued proudly, gesturing to the inky black tattoo which covered his wide bull-like neck. 'You're lucky you're just being locked up,' he continued, maliciously. 'Could've been whipped with the cat o' nine tails or made to walk the plank! Ah well,' he added, as if disappointed that these options had not been chosen. 'There's always tomorrow!' and with a horrible laugh, he pushed them all roughly inside, slammed the door and pushed home three bolts, leaving them in the gloom.

'And be quiet - or else!' he yelled through the wall.

The children looked at each other in the semi darkness. There were no windows, but they could hear the water a few metres below them, as well as the continued shouts from the celebrating pirates.

'So, that's vile Vinicius,' said Sam.

'Yeah,' replied Zav. 'This is a nice fix we've got ourselves into!'

'At least they didn't discover Ana and Demaria,' breathed Zelie, and Sofie gave her a hug.

'Thanks to your quick thinking!'

'Well, we may as well make ourselves as comfortable as we can,' said Sam practically. 'We should try and escape of course, but it will be better to try it at night.'

'I'll get Ana to take the message to Widow Hanlon that we've been kidnapped,' whispered Zelie. And she whistled the signal softly. They heard a light fluttering of wings outside and Zelie, her face pressed to the bamboo wall, whispered, 'Ana – tell Widow Hanlon what's happened. We need rescuing!'

'Roger that!' came the reply. 'Over and out!' A flutter of wings, and Ana had gone. A sudden yowl rent the air, and sharp claws ripped the side of the shack. Rattling Cat was still on the prowl, and she must have sensed Ana's presence. The children turned cold, but they heard a frustrated 'meow!' and the rattling of the bone necklace once more. Rattling Cat had been unsuccessful: Ana had escaped.

'Phew!' said Milo, shakily. 'I do NOT like that cat!'

'I won't call Demaria until later,' added Sofie shuddering. 'I can still hear that cat stalking around outside.'

Sam had been moving around the shack, meanwhile, checking for any weaknesses through which they might escape. 'Hello, what are these?' he wondered aloud, pointing to a bundle of papers in the corner.

'They look like charts!' exclaimed Zav, unrolling them. 'We should definitely take these with us when we escape!'

'And speaking of our escape,' Sam said, crouching in the corner of the shack, 'I reckon one of these floorboards is rotten! If we could help it on its way, we could drop down into the water and wade round the sides to the mouth of the cave!'

'The problem is, how are we going to loosen it with the pirates nearby and that horrid cat patrolling?' asked Sofie. 'We'll make too much noise and they'll know what we're up to!'

'Hmmm,' said Sam.

'Why don't we sing?' suggested Zelie? 'That would cover up the sound of you pushing the board through!'

'Great idea!' Sam replied. 'This could work! But we'll have to wait until it's darker – no good punching a hole in the floor and it being seen by the pirates!'

The children agreed that this was a sensible plan and settled down to wait for dusk. Time passed very slowly.

'I never really appreciated the illuminators before,' said Milo. 'It's so dark without them.'

'That's why it's so important to save Pa's power packs from the pirates,' Zelie reminded them. 'Imagine losing all the technology it has taken so many years to get back?'

Sam had pressed his eye to a crack in the wall and said,' Dusk is here! It'll be pitch black in a few minutes. Let's give it a go.'

He got into position, his foot above the rotting floor, ready to stamp down on it. The children started singing 'In the Quartermaster's Stores', memories of the last time they sung it on Captain Jett's boat filling their minds, boosting them to sing even more loudly than the drunken pirates. Sam managed a couple of hefty stamps before a roar cut through their singing. 'SHUT IT!' came Humberto's voice.

'Nearly there!' whispered Sam, 'one more chorus should do it!'

The others held hands and bravely launched into 'A Sailor Went to Sea, Sea, Sea' while Sam gave the board a last few hard stamps. He gave the thumbs up just as another roar rent the air.

'Pesky brats! Shut up or I will smash you!' And before the sleuths could respond, the shack shuddered as something with enormous force hit the side of it. Humberto had swung his vicious club at the shack. The structure swayed on its stilts, groaning.

'Next time that'll be your heads so when I say shut it, I mean SHUT. IT!' Humberto snarled, and he lumbered back to his guffawing pirate mates.

Sam was about to beckon the children over to the hole, when they heard a rattling sound that froze them in their tracks. Rattling Cat! She was still on patrol, and even if it was dark, the children knew they would never be able to sneak past her. Suddenly, Sofie sat bolt upright. 'Demaria!' she whispered. 'We can make her visible again and she can lead Rattling Cat off on a wild goose chase while we escape!'

'Brilliant,' said Sam. 'Let's do it.'

Sofie whistled for her parrot, and they knew she had arrived when they heard the snarling and swiping of very sharp claws from Rattling Cat. Sofie said, 'Demaria – be our decoy! Get rid of that cat!' and at the same time, Zelie muttered the magic words under her breath:

'Fairy fee, fairy fee, prevent invisibility!'

Ratting Cat yowled so loudly the children jumped! The next second, they heard the scrabbling of her claws and the frantic clanking of the bones swinging around her scrawny neck as she gave chase to the tantalising green parrot fluttering just centimetres out of her reach.

The children moved quickly towards the hole. 'Don't forget the charts!' hissed Zelie, and Sam stuffed them under his T-shirt.

'Right!' said Sam, 'I'll go down first as I'm the tallest. Zav you help the others down and I'll catch them at the bottom. Everybody - let's go!'

Taking a deep breath in case the water below was deeper than he'd thought, Sam jumped. He landed with a splash directly under the shack. Fortunately, the sound of yells coming from the rum-addled pirates meant he wasn't overheard. He looked up at the worried faces gazing down at him from the hole above and, giving them a double thumbs up, whispered, 'It's ok! Not too deep!' One by one they jumped down into the water.

The sleuths all joined hands, Sam leading and Zav bringing up the rear. They waded through the water, keeping to the side of the hurricane hole where they were hidden by shadows. It was tough going but they gritted their teeth and pushed on, keeping their eyes on the mouth of the cave and concentrating on pushing through the salty water one step at a time. They were soon shivering without the sun to warm them. Sam kept whispering encouraging words, 'And just think!' he said, 'going through water is the best way to make sure that nasty rattling cat can't follow us!'

'No scent to follow!' said Milo, his teeth chattering slightly.

'And cats hate water!' added Zelie.

After what seemed like hours, they finally reached the mouth of the cave where the pirate's lanterns could no longer be seen.

'It's lucky there's a full moon,' commented Zelie, 'we'd have found that much harder without it.'

'Yes, but we don't want the pirates to see us by it either' added Sam, frowning. 'Let's get out of the sea and hide behind the rocks. Then we can watch for a ship.' Sam clambered up the rock beckoning the others to follow. There was an indentation in the rocks where they could hunker down and dry off, unseen by anyone either in the cave or out to sea.

Meanwhile back at home in Red Port, Widow Hanlon was very worried. 'They know the rules,' she fretted to herself, 'they would never break them. Something has happened, these old bones of mine can feel it!'

Just then Ana swept in, 'Children in danger! Captured by pirates!'

Widow Hanlon clutched her hand to her heart, her face draining of colour. 'Mother of mercy!' she exclaimed. 'Fly to Captain Jett, Ana. We need ships. Do you know where the Captain is?'

'Yes,' Ana chirruped.

'Then fly like the wind!' With a flash of green, Ana flew off again, straight to Captain Jett aboard the Golden Ram.

'Pirates,' he said shortly to his First Mate as soon as Ana had delivered the news. 'Anchors away!' he cried. 'We'll head to Red Port first,' reaching for his charts. 'This island must be over here on this side,' he mused, pointing at the map, and Ana chirruped in confirmation. 'Mangroves,' Captain Jett continued grimly. 'A perfect hiding place. The channels are shallow around there, we'll have to use depth sounders to make sure we don't run aground and get stuck. Go and get the ropes ready,' he ordered his mate, as the proud ship pushed its way smoothly through the waves.

Back at the entrance to the hurricane hole the children were huddled behind the rocks.

'Which way will Captain Jett come in do you think?' asked Zav.

'I'm not sure,' Sam replied.

'Ana will show them the way,' said Zelie confidently.

'And Pa is an amazing sailor!' added Milo. 'I know he'll find us.'

'I'll call Demaria,' Sofie suggested. 'She can keep a look out!' She whistled and a few moments later, Demaria fluttered into view, landing on Sofie's shoulder and giving her an affectionate nip.

'Well done, Demaria!' Sofie said, 'you were brilliant getting rid of Rattling Cat!'

Demaria twittered happily, snuggling up to Sofie.

'Look!' cried Zav, jumping up and pointing. 'A ship!'

'Be careful!' said Zelie, pulling him back down. 'We don't know whose ship it is yet! If it's more pirates we definitely don't want them to know we're here.'

'I'll send Demaria to see,' suggested Sofie, and the parrot flew off. They then glimpsed another flash of green zoom up to meet her.

'Ana's there!' exclaimed Zelie.

'We're saved!' cried Zav, jumping up to perform a little victory dance. Demaria returned twittering excitedly, 'Captain Jett! Rescue! Jolly boat on the way!'

'Let's wade out so he can pick us up more easily,' suggested Sam.

The children slipped down the rocks in the moonlight, and waded into the water. They were hailed with a quiet, 'Ahoy me hearties!' from Old Pete who was at head of a rowing boat.

'Ahoy!' the children whispered back, grinning, and the strong arms of the sailors hauled them inside.

Captain Jett's smiling face greeted them, and he gave them all a big bear hug. 'What on earth have you lot been up to?' he asked.

'Oh, just bits and bobs!' replied Zelie airily, and the children burst out laughing. Suddenly, a furious roar ripped through the air, coming straight from the hurricane hole.

'Looks like they've discovered our escape,' said Sam. 'We got away just in time.'

'Well, they'll soon have a lot more to shout about,' said Captain Jett grimly. 'Back up ships are on the way to arrest them all. Old Pete will take you home.'

'Can't we stay and see the capture?' Zav asked.

'Absolutely not,' replied the Captain. 'It's far too dangerous and we're not attempting it until dawn when we can see what's happening and we have back up. Anyway, I think you've had quite enough adventures for one night!' he added, ruffling Milo's hair.

***

'Thank goodness you're home safe!' exclaimed Widow Hanlon a short time later as she hugged all the children in turn, ushering them into the kitchen where a big pan of delicious smelling soup waited on the stove.

'The only problem with sleuthing,' commented Zav as he eagerly tucked in, 'is the lack of sustenance.'

'True!' the others agreed, their mouths full.

'Oh, go on with you!' said Widow Hanlon, rolling her eyes and taking a friendly swipe at Zav with her tea towel.

The children grinned at each other.

'Well, we've officially been Super Sleuths and solved our first case,' remarked Zelie.

'Yes!' agreed Milo. 'What shall we call it?'

'The Case of the Pirates' Plunder!' replied Zav, and he held his cup of iced mango juice aloft, crying, 'Here's to many more!'

The children clinked their glasses and took deep, thirsty gulps.

'That was a very exciting day,' observed Sofie, 'But I'm glad to be home safe!'

'Me too,' agreed Milo, stifling a yawn.

'To bed with yous!' said Widow Hanlon. 'There'll be no more news until the morning,' she added, looking firmly at Sam who seemed about to protest. He shrugged, smiled at her and stood up, stretching.

'Thank you!' said Zelie hugging Widow Hanlon. 'We missed you, Hanni!'

'Get along now, Missie!' the cook replied, her brusque manner not quite managing to hide how relieved she was that they were all back in one piece.

The next morning when they woke up there was bad news. The pirates had been captured but Vile Vinicius had vanished and so had Humberto.

'We'll need to call him Vanished Vile Vinicius,' joked Captain Jett grimly.

'It wasn't your fault he got away Pa,' said Milo. 'If you'd gone in at night lots of people would have died.'

'We got the power packs back and all the crew of the ship. The Moving Way's been saved!' said Zav. 'Pa will be pleased.'

'The other pirates have been captured too,' added Sam, 'and that's a good thing for everyone.'

The pirates had been tight lipped about the plunder when questioned.

'They have their own code and will tell us nothing.' Captain Jett explained, 'but they are all members of the Black Cross Gang as they have the same tattoo. Unfortunately, we'll never get information out of the House of Vendetta - they're more afraid of whoever is behind this than they are of us. The only good news is that they are starting the charts of the area north of Red Cove so we'll be able to explore the bay. It'll be one less place for pirates to hide.'

'Isn't it good we took the charts we found!' said Zav. 'They'll help with the mapping.'

'Yes, they will,' Captain Jett continued, 'and there's something else. Here's an invitation to the palace for all of you. The King wishes to thank you personally.'

'Great, we can meet Richenda again,' said Zelie. 'You can meet her too,' she said to Sam and Sofie. 'You'll really like her - and Clarence!'

A few days later the sleuths arrived at the Palace of the Flowers They were taken into the huge throne room, where all important events took place. There was the sound of trumpets as they entered and royal banners were unfurled. Guards in livery beckoned them towards King Lucio and Queen Aurelia who were sitting on their ornate golden thrones with Princess Richenda standing beside them. The King rose from his throne and so did everybody else.

'Thank you for your help,' King Lucio announced to the sleuths. 'You've done very well and saved the Moving Way. The people of Sandlandia have much to praise you for.'

They bowed in response.

The King then called out each of the sleuths in turn and they walked forward so the king could present them with a medal as a reward. The shining medallions were hung proudly around their necks.

'They're real gold!' thought Sam, excited to have some plunder of his own.

'We are also very grateful for the charts you have found of the area,' continued King Lucio. 'Mapping is very difficult but these will help Captain Jett investigate the channels north of Red Cove.'

'We do hope you'll see Richenda more often, she could do with some company,' added Queen Aurelia. The children all smiled, nodding vigorously in agreement.

Later as the sleuths enjoyed another celebratory feast in the golden pavilion, Richenda seemed preoccupied.

'What's the matter?' asked Sofie.

'Is it the house of Contuti?' asked Zelie, following Richenda's gaze to where Count Zuto and Countess Rosina sat.

'No, it's Prince Igor.'

'He's here?'

'Yes, he's the big man over there with the Contutis.'

The sleuths looked and at the head of the table a huge shape sat stuffing pastries into his mouth. On his shoulder sat a dazzling white bird whose cold eyes swept the pavilion.

'He looks horrid,' said Milo. 'Is he staying long?'

'Yes,' replied Richenda glumly, 'and he really scares me! That bird is sinister.'

The sleuths nodded. They thought so too

'Don't be scared, 'said Sofie, giving her a hug.

'I don't want to go back to my lonely life,' the princess continued sadly.

'You won't be lonely any more now you know us,' replied Zelie. 'We can see each other in the city. Well, Zav and Milo and I can and we can come to your aid as well if you need it.'

'Thank you,' sniffed Richenda. 'I know you would, but how would I summon you?'

'Light the bonfire or ring the bell,' grinned Zav.

'Don't be silly - the whole city would be alerted and think it was a pirate attack,' said Zelie.

'Pa's got a new invention called a talker-listener. We'll bring you one!' suggested Zav.

'Great idea!' said Milo.

'And I'll send Ana up to see you with secret messages!' added Zelie. 'You're one of us now, Richenda - and Super Sleuths stick together.' Zelie grinned at the others.

Elementary,' said Zav.

'My dear Watson!' chorused the others.

"The End"

Have you listened to this book read aloud via our podcast? It's free on iTunes and on the Acast app.

Read by Lexi, don't miss it!

You can also visit us at our website www.supersleuths.net and explore the world of Sandlandia!

Enjoyed 'Super Sleuths and the Pirate's Plunder'? Please leave us a review. See you next time!

Zelie, Milo, Zav, Sofie and Sam

Printed in Great Britain
by Amazon

80572697R00058